Hidden Pictures

Nancy Drew DIARIES™

Hidden Pictures

#19

CAROLYN KEENE

Aladdin

NEW YORK   LONDON   TORONTO   SYDNEY   NEW DELHI

ALADDIN

An imprint of Simon & Schuster Children's Publishing Division
1230 Avenue of the Americas, New York, New York 10020
First Aladdin paperback edition January 2020
Text copyright © 2020 by Simon & Schuster, Inc.
Cover illustration copyright © 2020 by Erin McGuire
Also available in an Aladdin hardcover edition.
All rights reserved, including the right of reproduction in whole or in part in any form.
ALADDIN and related logo are registered trademarks of Simon & Schuster, Inc.
NANCY DREW, NANCY DREW DIARIES, and related logo are
trademarks of Simon & Schuster, Inc.
For information about special discounts for bulk purchases, please contact
Simon & Schuster Special Sales at 1-866-506-1949 or business@simonandschuster.com.
The Simon & Schuster Speakers Bureau can bring authors to your live event.
For more information or to book an event contact the Simon & Schuster Speakers Bureau
at 1-866-248-3049 or visit our website at www.simonspeakers.com.
Series designed by Karin Paprocki
Cover designed by Heather Palisi
Interior designed by Mike Rosamilia
The text of this book was set in Adobe Caslon Pro.
Manufactured in the United States of America 1219 OFF
2 4 6 8 10 9 7 5 3 1
Library of Congress Cataloging-in-Publication Data
Names: Keene, Carolyn, author.
Title: Hidden pictures / by Carolyn Keene.
Description: First Aladdin hardcover/paperback edition. |
New York : Aladdin, 2020. | Series: Nancy Drew diaries ; #19 |
Summary: In the sleepy town of Shady Oaks, Nancy Drew and her friends investigate an exhibit of
photographs, rumored to be cursed, and their connection to the disappearance of two people. |
Identifiers: LCCN 2019003847 (print) | LCCN 2019006508 (eBook) |
ISBN 9781534421042 (eBook) | ISBN 9781534421028 (pbk) | ISBN 9781534421035 (hardcover)
Subjects: | CYAC: Photographs—Fiction. | Museums—Fiction. | Missing persons—Fiction. |
Blessing and cursing—Fiction. | Mystery and detective stories.
Classification: LCC PZ7.K23 (eBook) | LCC PZ7.K23 Hf 2020 (print) |
DDC [Fic]—dc23
LC record available at https://lccn.loc.gov/2019003847

Contents

Dear Diary,

YOU WOULD THINK A TOWN AS SMALL as Shady Oaks wouldn't have too much going on. At least that's what I thought, before I was sent a mysterious newspaper clipping about the town museum's newest exhibit. Apparently, one of the museum's employees has gone missing, only to show up in one of the photographs on display!

   Now I have to know: Who sent me this article and why? Is someone tampering with the exhibit? Or is the explanation a bit more supernatural? According to the article, the photographs are rumored to be cursed. But I'm sure I don't believe in curses. . . .

CHAPTER ONE

It's Raining Suspicion

"HEY, NANCY!" BESS CALLED TO ME FROM across the street. "This is him, right? The photographer?"

George and I made our way over to where Bess was standing. She was looking in the front window of an arts and crafts store, where there was a printout of a large black-and-white photograph. The photo was of a serious-looking man with heavy wrinkles, dark hair, and wide, light gray eyes. Or at least they looked gray, since the photograph had no color.

"Right," I said. "That's Christopher DeSantos."

We were in the town of Shady Oaks, a drive of

several hours from River Heights. It was fall and there were trees everywhere, shading the town with red, orange, and yellow leaves that were covering everything like one large umbrella. Lining the main street were lampposts, and each of them was draped with a banner for the Carlisle Museum and the new exhibit featuring pictures of Shady Oaks by the world-famous photographer Christopher DeSantos. DeSantos had grown up in town and spent his teenage years taking pictures. None of these photographs had ever been seen before. They had all been donated only recently by DeSantos's granddaughter, who had lived here with her grandfather after his retirement. She had moved to Shady Oaks when she was only a child, over twenty years ago, but she had apparently never left.

"He looks . . . ," began George, before eventually finding the right word. "Intimidating."

"It's probably just the photograph," said Bess. "If the lighting were different and if he was smiling, he wouldn't look so . . ."

"Frightening?" George tried again.

"Well, yes," said Bess.

Bess and George were my best friends, but they couldn't be more different. That much was clear just by looking at them. It was raining lightly in Shady Oaks and Bess had brought along a pair of polka-dotted rain boots, pulled up carefully over her jeans, and a matching polka-dotted umbrella. Her blond hair was tucked behind her ears and protected entirely from the rain. George, on the other hand, had thrown on an oversize green parka. She had pulled the hood down low over her forehead, but tufts of her dark hair still peeked out from underneath it and were slowly soaking up rainwater.

Personally, I had opted for something more in the middle. I was wearing my red raincoat, zipped up to protect me from the wind, a warm cable-knit sweater, and a pair of boots.

"So where to now?" said Bess, turning away from the window. "Should we find the museum?"

"No way," said George. "No museums until after breakfast."

"I agree," I said. "We should definitely get some food first."

Truthfully, I was eager to find the Carlisle Museum and visit the new Christopher DeSantos exhibit. But we had driven to Shady Oaks and checked into our hotel pretty late last night. No restaurants had been open, and I would have felt bad making my friends wait to eat this morning. Especially since I knew neither of them were very interested in Christopher DeSantos, or even photography in general.

We continued walking down the main street. Bess was trying to avoid puddles as she went. I was on the lookout for other potential museumgoers. Shady Oaks seemed pretty busy. Despite the rain and the small size of the town, there were actually a good number of people walking around. Many of the stores had window displays advertising the DeSantos exhibit, and most of the pedestrians were stopping to look at each one. I had to assume we were surrounded by tourists and DeSantos fans.

George had fallen a few steps behind us. She had

taken out her cell phone and was holding it up in the air as she looked for service. I could see the droplets of water already collecting on her phone screen.

"No cell service!" she called to us. She sounded a bit miserable. "And no Wi-Fi at the hotel. Why did we come to such a remote town again?"

Next to me, Bess rolled her eyes. "George," she called back. "Nancy is a big fan of Christopher DeSantos! As her friends, we should be happy to tag along so she gets to experience this. Right, Nancy?"

"Um," I said. "Right. Thanks, Bess."

I knew I wasn't being very convincing. Especially when Bess turned toward me and looked a little confused. "Nancy," she said. "You *are* a DeSantos fan, aren't you?"

"Well," I said. The truth was, I hadn't even heard of Christopher DeSantos or his photographs until a couple of days ago. There was another reason I wanted to visit Shady Oaks. But before I could explain what we were really doing there, I saw someone walking toward us.

"Hello!" the person called out. She was wearing a bright yellow raincoat, and her intensely red hair was pulled back into a ponytail that flicked behind her as she walked. Around her neck she carried what looked like an old-fashioned film camera, but it was encased in a clear plastic covering, to protect it from the rain. "Are you guys here for the exhibit? Are you huge Christopher DeSantos fans too?"

"That's what we were just wondering," said Bess.

The girl looked confused, so I quickly held my hand out to her. "Yes," I said. "We're all big fans. I'm Nancy, this is Bess, and that's George, with the cell phone."

At the sound of her name, George looked over at us and the new girl. She waved as she walked over to join us.

"I'm Riley," said the girl. She smiled, and I could see that she had slightly buck teeth and that her nose was dotted with freckles. "I've been waiting for this exhibit to open for months. Are you guys staying in town?"

"Yes," said Bess, smiling back at her. "At the Elder Root Inn." Leave it to Bess to be unfailingly polite, even when I knew she was dying to ask me what was really going on.

"Oh, me too!" said Riley. "It's just so exciting to meet other fans."

"Nancy's the fan," said George, who had come up to stand on my right side. "Not me or Bess."

Riley looked between us, clearly confused again, since I had just told her we were all fans of DeSantos's work. Before I could get our story straight, George continued on.

"I just don't understand why anyone would continue to use a film camera when digital exists," she said. She looked pointedly at what was hanging from Riley's neck.

"George!" said Bess, but luckily, Riley only laughed.

"You'd be surprised how different they are," she said. "I'd be happy to show you. But of course, DeSantos shot using only film, and his work speaks for itself. Right, Nancy?"

"Of course," I said, a little sheepishly.

"I think his series on Copper Canyon would have been impossible to capture with digital," said Riley. "And those are probably some of my favorite pieces. What about you? What's your favorite DeSantos photograph?"

"Um—uh—well—" I stammered. Riley, Bess, and George were all looking at me, but really, I couldn't have named a single DeSantos photograph if I wanted to.

Just at that moment, a single, piercing scream turned our attention down the street. As I looked in the direction from which it had come, I saw what seemed to be some kind of commotion in front of a large brick building. A sign on it clearly read THE CARLISLE MUSEUM—the same museum that was hosting the photographs of Christopher DeSantos.

CHAPTER TWO

The Second Victim

I LOOKED QUICKLY AT BESS AND GEORGE before we all took off, jogging down the street and in the direction of whoever had screamed. We made it to the museum before I realized that Riley had tagged along as well.

We weren't the only ones to hear the scream and wonder what was happening. A few people who appeared as though they had been walking past the museum had stopped to check on the sudden sound. There was also a park nearby, and I could see a few people lifting up the hoods of their raincoats or readjusting their umbrellas so they could see what was happening as they walked through.

There were two women standing on the museum's front steps. One of them looked as though she was maybe a year or two older than me. She had light brown hair that was parted in the middle and hung straight down. Her hand was covering her mouth, and she was crying. It must have been she who had screamed. I watched as she began gesturing at anyone who was nearby.

"You have to listen to me!" she kept calling out. "Please, I need help!"

The second woman on the museum steps looked as though she was trying to calm the girl down, or at least move her back inside. This woman was thin, with short white hair and hunched shoulders. She was wearing a navy-blue blazer, and pinned to it was a name tag. I had to assume she worked for the museum.

Nearly everyone who had been in listening distance made their way over, and soon the two women were surrounded by a small crowd of people. The girl started motioning back through the open door of the museum, though it wasn't immediately clear why. I left Bess, George, and Riley behind and edged my way to the front of the crowd.

"Come here, dear," the older woman said. "Let's move over this way."

The crying girl wouldn't budge, and more people were gathering around her.

"What's happening?" someone from the crowd asked her.

This question had clearly been what the girl was waiting for. She began speaking loudly, addressing the crowd. "My boyfriend," she began. "He's missing. He's trapped in there."

"Trapped in the museum?" said someone else. "What do you mean?"

If the girl had been nearly hysterical before, now she seemed to be determined and almost calm. "We were visiting the museum last night," she said. "My boyfriend and I. But then he just disappeared. I thought that maybe he was just going to meet me back at our hotel or something. But he never showed. So I came back to the museum this morning, to look for him, and I found him. It's the same thing that happened to that other girl, last week. They're both trapped inside the exhibit, inside the photographs!"

There was a mix of different reactions throughout the crowd. One woman laughed, clearly thinking this was a joke. Some gasped, while others just looked confused. But the woman who worked at the museum didn't look surprised at all. Instead she looked worried.

The crying girl continued. "It's the curse!" she said, this time looking around at everyone gathered in the crowd. "Terry Lawrence cursed these photographs, and they're going to keep taking people until the exhibit is shut down."

The museum worker stepped forward, waving her hands in front of herself as if she were trying to quiet the girl down. "No, no," she said. Her voice sounded a bit wheezy and strained. "We aren't shutting down and there is no curse. Absolutely no such thing as a curse. Someone is just tampering with my exhibit."

The crying girl looked as though she was about to respond to this when a police officer began making his way through the crowd. He was a short man, with heavy cheeks and a rounded nose. "What's going on here?" he called out to the two women.

"Officer!" said the crying girl. "You have to help me. My boyfriend's missing. He's trapped inside a DeSantos photograph. This exhibit is cursed and needs to be shut down immediately!"

I watched the officer closely, wondering how he would react. I expected that he might look confused or unsure, but to my surprise he rolled his eyes and only appeared to be slightly bored.

"Susan," he said, turning toward the woman who worked for the museum. "We've already told you. You have to put a stop to this little stunt of yours. You can't fake a curse in order to get more publicity. It's *fraud*."

The museum worker, Susan, began shaking her head rapidly. "I have nothing to do with the missing people," she said. "I wouldn't be involved in something like that."

"This is real," insisted the crying girl. "And so is the curse."

Now the police officer did look unsure. He glanced between the women as if one of them might break and admit they were lying. Neither of them said anything, though, so the police officer suggested, "How about we get both of your statements, all right? Down at the police station."

Both women nodded and allowed themselves to be shepherded off to the side of the building and, eventually, into the police car parked nearby.

The officer then returned to where the crowd was still gathered and asked everyone to head home, or at least to clear away from the steps. As people began to move, I felt myself being jostled by the crowd. A few people bumped into my shoulders. I knew Bess and George were back behind me, but instead of heading toward them, I slipped through everyone else into the museum.

Unlike the outside of the museum, with its weathered red brick, the inside of the museum was painted a clean white. It was also empty. No museum staff were there to stop me as I followed signs to the room with the DeSantos exhibit, just off the main lobby. There were sharp spotlights everywhere in the exhibit space, and most were directed at the photographs on the wall. The seating was minimal, just a few plain benches spread out around the room.

It didn't take long to find what I was looking for. The screaming woman had been correct: there was something very out of place in one of the photographs. It was one of an older-looking Shady Oaks, and the little card below it said it had been taken in 1945. The strange part was in the background, because there was also a man wearing a hoodie and jeans, clearly modern-day clothing. He was walking through a group of people wearing 1940s clothing. His head was turned so he was looking back over his shoulder. He was frozen midstep. He must be the crying woman's boyfriend.

I was looking at the photograph so intently that I didn't even hear Bess and George come up behind me.

"Nancy?" said Bess, from over my shoulder. "I think you have some explaining to do."

The museum quickly filled up with other people from the crowd wanting to see the impossible photographs. I knew it wasn't going to be a good place to talk, so I told Bess and George we should go back to our original plan. We would find a place to eat breakfast, and I would tell them everything.

On our way out, I also spotted Riley and invited her along. Bess and George both gave me a strange look, probably wondering why I would want to talk about any of this in front of someone we had just met. I needed information, though, and I was willing to bet Riley could tell me a lot about Christopher DeSantos.

We found a diner just a little ways downtown. The rain had let up, but the diner's windows were still all fogged. Inside the building, the foggy windows and the wood paneling and the smell of pancakes made everything feel cozy and warm. We all happily shed our rain gear. Riley and I were sitting on one side of a vinyl booth, while Bess and George sat on the other. By the time we had all ordered and had our hands wrapped around mugs of hot chocolate, Bess and George were ready to ask some questions.

"All right, Nancy," said Bess. "What's going on?"

"I'm not really a Christopher DeSantos fan," I said, hunching my shoulders. I felt guilty about having lied to my friends, even if I had a good reason.

"That much is obvious," said George, blowing away the steam rising from her mug.

"But we hadn't found a good mystery in forever!" I explained. "And then someone sent me this."

I pulled a folded piece of paper from my back pocket. It was a newspaper clipping, now heavily creased and slightly wrinkled. The headline read, IMAGE OF MISSING GIRL APPEARS AT DESANTOS EXHIBIT. And printed in black and white was a grainy photograph of the Carlisle Museum.

"One of the museum employees, a girl named Grace Rogers, disappeared a week ago," I said. "But the image of her did appear in one of the DeSantos photographs. Which is impossible, since all the photographs in the exhibit are from the 1940s. The article says that the photographs are supposedly cursed, and that every person who has tried to display a DeSantos photograph has had something terrible happen to them."

"And no one has tried to shut down the exhibit?" asked Bess. "What about the police?"

I shook my head. "According to the article, the police here have already debunked the curse once. The curator at the Carlisle Museum, who I'm guessing is the white-haired woman we just saw, tried to fake the curse when the exhibit was first announced. She claimed one of the photographs had disappeared, when really she'd just hidden it away. Even after Grace vanished, the police still maintained that Susan was behind it. The article says that they're giving her until Friday to admit that she and her employee, the missing girl, planned this entire thing. That's three days from now. If they don't come forward, the police are going to close the museum." I paused, then added thoughtfully,

"And now that there's a second victim, who knows what the police will do?"

Bess and George each took a turn scanning the newspaper clipping.

Riley read it through too, seemingly just as curious as we were. "I've heard about the curse before, of course," she told us. "But I hadn't heard about the earlier disappearance. Who sent you this article?"

"I have no idea, but I think they want me to figure out whatever is going on here before the museum closes," I said. "It was just too good of a mystery to resist."

Eventually Bess said, "It *is* very interesting. But I wish you'd just been honest with us."

"I agree," said George. "Anyway, this makes way more sense than your sudden interest in photography."

"So," I said cautiously, "does that mean we can stay and solve this?"

Bess and George looked at each other and seemed to reach a decision without saying anything at all. They turned back to me, and both smiled and nodded.

"As long as you agree to tell us everything from here on out," said Bess.

"Definitely," I agreed. "It's a promise." I meant it, and I also felt a surge of affection for my two best friends. Not just anyone would stay with me and help solve this mystery, but Bess and George were special.

"So you're a detective?" asked Riley. She was still holding the newspaper clipping and looking around at the three of us. "Not a fan?"

"Sorry, Riley," said Nancy. "I'm not a fan. But you are, and I was hoping I could ask you a few questions."

"Sure," said Riley, taking a slurping sip of her drink. "What do you want to know?"

I smiled. I had a good feeling about Riley and I knew she would want to help, especially once she knew there were people missing.

"First," I said, "I want to know what exactly this curse is, and where the idea came from." I had researched the curse online, and the article I was sent contained some information as well. But nothing seemed to match up, and all my sources had a different story. I knew I needed to talk to someone in person.

"Oh," said Riley, leaning in closer and lowering her voice. "Well, it's just a rumor. But did you know Christopher DeSantos used to have a work partner?"

I nodded. I had read a few things about Christopher DeSantos's career online. "His name was Terry Lawrence," I said.

"Right," said Riley. "For about two decades, he and DeSantos traveled together and took photographs of the same landscapes. But in the 1970s they had a falling-out. There was this photograph that became incredibly famous, and they both claimed to have taken it. You see, they were so close they shared a darkroom. The film somehow got mislabeled or mixed up. They were never able to agree on the truth, and it ended their friendship. DeSantos ultimately got the credit for it, but nobody really knows for sure. And personally, I think all the gossip eclipsed how good the photograph actually was."

"And the curse?" I asked.

"Soon after the two of them stopped working together," Riley said, "Terry Lawrence did an interview where he claimed to have cursed Christopher DeSantos's entire collection of work. He said that anyone who attempted to display any of his photographs would have something horrible happen to them. And for a while, that's just what happened. One museum caught fire. Another lost all its funding and had to shut down. And one more had a member of its staff go missing. They were never found."

"Like what's happening now," I said. Riley nodded. "And people think Terry Lawrence was actually capable of all that? That he could curse something?"

"I know it's weird," Riley said. "No one believed him at first, of course. But after all that . . ."

"Didn't people think that Terry did all those things? To make it seem like the curse was real?" George asked.

"Some people did, but the police were never able to confirm it," Riley explained. "He always had airtight alibis."

"So what about now? Would Terry Lawrence have anything to do with this?" asked Bess.

"Yeah," said George. "He could be trying to sabotage this exhibit, right?"

"Oh," said Riley. "No. Terry Lawrence died years ago. Years before Christopher DeSantos, even."

George slumped back in her seat. "So that's a dead end," she said.

"Can you think of anyone still living who might want to sabotage the exhibit?" I asked.

"And who would be willing to kidnap people in order to do it," added Bess.

Riley's eyes went wide and she said, "Actually, yes. And she even lives in town."

"Who?" Bess, George, and I all asked at once.

At first Riley looked a little nervous about what she was going to say. But eventually she grinned conspiratorially and said, "I wouldn't be surprised if Beverly DeSantos had something to do with it. Christopher DeSantos's granddaughter."

"Beverly DeSantos?" I asked. "Isn't she the one who

found and donated all the photographs to the museum in the first place?"

"Well, yeah," said Riley. "But it's pretty well known that she never liked her grandfather. She even once said in an interview that she wished she had been born into a different family. It's very possible that she still holds a grudge against him. In the interview, Beverly said—"

Just then Riley stopped talking. All the color drained from her face, and I saw that she was looking at something behind Bess and George.

I looked up. There had been a woman in the booth in front of us, but we were only able to see the back of her head. Now she was suddenly standing and looking right at us. Her long dark hair hung loose around her shoulders, and her dense eyebrows were drawn together, like she was thinking hard about something. She had a thick curtain of bangs, and I couldn't help but feel like the rest of her face was hiding behind them. Her eyes were light in color, and they looked vaguely familiar.

"Riley?" Bess asked.

Riley just shook her head and wouldn't say anything else. I didn't actually know what Beverly DeSantos looked like, but I was willing to guess she was the woman standing right in front of us. And she had been close to enough to hear our entire conversation.

CHAPTER THREE

The Hidden Doorway

BEVERLY DESANTOS DID NOT STAY OR attempt to confront us. There was a long pause as she continued to look in our direction. Then she turned around and headed outside, the door sweeping in a gust of cold wind behind her.

"Was that . . . ?" asked George, looking back at Riley.

Riley nodded slowly. "Yes," she said. "That was Beverly DeSantos."

"It's possible she didn't hear that, though," said Bess sympathetically. "Right, George? Nancy?"

Neither George nor I answered. It was pretty clear that Beverly DeSantos had heard everything, and Riley seemed to know it too. Looking at Riley, I couldn't tell if she was more embarrassed at being overheard or frightened of becoming the next kidnapping victim if Beverly really was staging a curse. The color had yet to come back to Riley's face, and she no longer seemed to feel like answering our questions.

Eventually Riley stood and told us she wasn't feeling that hungry anymore. "I think I'm going to head back to the hotel," she said. "I need . . ." She took a break here, as if she was thinking of what to say next. "Something for my camera," she finally said.

"Of course," I said, even though I didn't really believe her. "Thank you for your help, Riley."

She smiled at that and seemed genuinely pleased to have assisted us. "If it'll help you find the missing people, then it was worth it," she said. "I just hope I'm not next."

"You won't be," I promised.

The fabric of Riley's yellow raincoat squeaked

against itself as she put her hands through the sleeves. "Thanks, Nancy," she said. "I'll see you guys later."

Not long after Riley had stepped out through the front door, our food came: Bess's french toast and fresh fruit, George's stack of pancakes, and my omelet and toast. Riley's scrambled eggs came as well, even though Riley was long gone. Bess happily ate them herself.

When our food was nearly gone, Bess turned to me and said, "So what do we do now?"

I already had a plan. "Well," I said, "I want to head back to the museum to get a good look at both photographs: the one with Grace Rogers, which I didn't get to see earlier, and the one from this morning, with that girl's boyfriend. Maybe there are some clues, or something I missed during my first look."

Bess and George nodded.

"And if it's possible," I continued, "I'd like to find that girl from this morning and talk to her. The one who was crying in front of the museum."

"She went to the police station, right?" asked

George, around a final bite of pancake. "To be questioned. Should we go there?"

Bess rolled her eyes at George's table manners. But really, George was correct.

"Right," I said. "I'm guessing she'll be there awhile. So the museum, and then the police station."

We finished up our meals and headed outside. The rain hadn't started again, but the sky was a dark gray and it looked as though it might pour at any moment. George pulled the hood of her parka up over her head as a precaution, and Bess had her umbrella shut but still at the ready, just in case. I left my hood down and my raincoat unzipped. I don't mind a little rain.

We reached the museum after just a short walk. Word must have spread about all the excitement earlier this morning, because the museum was now packed with people.

We weren't able to just slip inside this time. We each bought a ticket, which would be good for the entire week, and headed over to the exhibit to try and look at the photographs. But this was more difficult than it sounded. There were people everywhere. The few benches inside the exhibit room were all crammed full of museumgoers, practically sitting on each other's laps, and it was difficult to even move around the exhibit's small space.

The most crowded sections by far were the spaces in front of the two photographs containing the missing people. Everyone seemed to want to see the impossible pictures, and I was sure the upset this morning must have really boosted ticket sales.

"Hey," I said, turning to face Bess and George. "How about I try and get a closer look, and you two can just hang back? It'll be easier for one person to make it through that crowd than three."

Bess and George both looked relieved at that suggestion. They were hunching into each other and unsuccessfully trying to dodge the shoulders of all the people around them.

"Sounds great," said Bess.

"Yeah," George added. "Thanks, Nancy."

"No problem," I said as I left them behind and headed into the densest part of the crowd.

From everything I'd researched about Christopher DeSantos's work, I knew he mainly focused on landscapes. He was especially well known for capturing national parks and other parts of the natural world not many people were able to actually visit. But the photographs in this exhibit were different. These were all of Shady Oaks in the 1940s, mainly images of the streets and the storefronts and portraits of the people who must have been living there at the time. They seemed to me less like professional work and more like a personal portrayal of the town where this man had lived, both when he was young and after he had retired.

Even though I don't know much about photography, I could quickly tell that the photographs where DeSantos captured people were my favorites. It was almost like each image contained clues about who that person really was, and each person had been made into a mystery to be solved.

Eventually I managed to get close enough to the

photograph containing the image of Grace Rogers to get a good look at it. Like the image of the crying girl's boyfriend, this photo showed Grace in the background of the photograph, like she had just happened to be walking through it when the picture was taken. She too was wearing modern-day clothing. The image wasn't very clear, but it looked as though she was wearing a blazer, which would make sense, since she was a museum employee.

The image of Grace also seemed to have the same coloring and texture as the rest of the photograph. It didn't look like a separate image at all. Finally, I could also see that there appeared to be a lock on the side of the frame, preventing anyone from taking the photograph—which made sense for an art museum. I couldn't tell how someone might have tampered with the photograph, but I tried to commit every detail to memory just in case they would prove helpful later.

I made my way over to the second photograph, the one of the crying girl's boyfriend, by cutting through the crowds once more. The photograph looked nearly the same as the one of Grace. I couldn't see any flaw in the image; it really did look like he was walking through the background. And like the photograph of Grace, there was a lock on the side of the frame, protected by a combination. A quick glance around was all I needed to confirm that the other photographs in the exhibit were similarly protected by locking frames.

After I felt satisfied with my investigation, I made my way back to where I had left Bess and George. It wasn't easy, even though I was now trying to move farther away from the photographs instead of closer to them. Everyone in the crowd seemed just as unwilling to let me through.

I couldn't have been gone more than twenty minutes, but by the time I got back to where Bess and George had been, they were gone. I quickly looked around. I didn't recognize anyone. There were a few children running around, boys who must have been around five or six and who were playing tag. There was an older couple, sitting on one of the benches and leaning against each other. There were a lot of people with cameras like Riley's. I assumed they were all fans who had traveled to Shady Oaks to see this exhibit. But I didn't see Bess or George anywhere, and for a moment I panicked and wondered if they had been trapped inside the photographs as well. I quickly pulled myself together. Of course that was impossible. People do not get trapped in photographs, and I would just have to look around in order to find my friends.

I stuck to the outer edges of the room, especially the places where there were no photographs, as these were the least populated areas. If Bess and George were still here, I knew they would have kept to these places, anywhere where there weren't too many people.

I wasn't having much luck. Bess and George must have left the museum altogether. I was about to go outside when I realized something else interesting. From the outside, the museum had looked gigantic. It was easily the largest building on the block, much taller and wider than the small stores surrounding it. But the room set aside for the exhibit was incredibly small. There didn't seem to be any way to reach the other sections of the museum, or signs for any other exhibits.

I could only see one door besides the one at the room's entrance. It was marked STAFF ONLY.

I looked around. No one was paying much attention to me. Everyone was too distracted by the DeSantos photographs, both the impossible ones and the ordinary ones that had not been tampered with, which were distracting enough in their own right. I made my way over and snuck through the door.

It wasn't as interesting as I had hoped. I found myself in what appeared to be a hallway that also doubled as storage. There were four doors leading off from the hallway, and each of them was shut.

I walked forward slowly, trying to be as quiet as possible, just in case any of the doors led to occupied rooms. The hallway was cluttered with items that appeared to be left over from old displays and other objects from previous exhibits. There were old signs and banners and a large bookshelf pushed against the wall at the end of the hallway. Most everything in here was covered with a thick layer of dust, and I could guess that most of these things had not been used in a long time. I could see other locking frames, like the ones currently hanging in the DeSantos exhibit, except these were leaning up against the wall and all different sizes. Some of them were tiny, while others were taller than I was.

I spent a moment looking at the mechanisms that locked the frames. They were all the same kind of lock that I had seen in the exhibit. If someone wanted to take whatever was within one of these frames, they would need to know the combination.

Cautiously I began opening the doors leading off from the hallway. The two doors closest to me both contained small offices, likewise filled with props from old exhibits. Next there was a storage closet, and finally a closet filled with cleaning supplies. But these were all small rooms and didn't explain all the extra space that must have been somewhere else in the museum.

I was about to give up and go back out through the STAFF ONLY door, when I looked down at the floor and noticed something interesting. The closer you were to the walls of the hallway, the dustier the floor became. This was true everywhere except the far wall where the bookcase was. There was a clear rectangle of not-dusty floor just to the right of the bookcase. I was willing to bet that was where the bookcase had previously been standing, and that someone must have recently moved it.

I walked quickly over to the bookcase and checked everything that was on it. There wasn't much. Old lights and some smaller frames. I leaned around to look behind the bookcase, and hiding behind it was another door. I knew there had to be more to this museum!

There was just enough space between the bookcase and the wall that I could squeeze in between them, and hopefully open that door. I began sidestepping and reaching toward the door handle. I was completely behind the bookcase before I realized how much dust I had stirred up. It was floating all around me. But I still managed to get my hand on the door handle and it was—locked.

The light wasn't great back there, but I could just make out a keypad above the door handle. It seemed that everything in this museum was locked through the use of combinations. If I wanted to get through, I would need to figure out the numerical code specific to this door.

I began to step sideways in the other direction, ready to get out of there, when I heard a door shut behind me. There was someone else in the hallway with me.

Actually, there were two people. I stood still where I was hiding, careful not to make a sound, and I could hear them arguing.

"I'm sorry," said one of the voices. "But I just can't help you." The voice was breathy and wheezy, and I realized I recognized it. It was the woman from this morning, Susan, who worked at the museum.

"You have to," said the other voice. This one sounded much more steady, and it was also loud, and the speaker was clearly upset. "Do you know what people are already saying? That the photographs are cursed. I overheard someone, some girl, this morning at the diner."

Oh no. I was willing to bet that the girl they were talking about was none other than Riley. That would mean that this other voice must belong to Beverly DeSantos.

"There's no such thing as curses," said the museum worker.

"It doesn't matter if—"

But I didn't get to hear whatever it was that Beverly DeSantos thought didn't matter. Because just then, all the dust floating around finally got to me. I couldn't help but sneeze.

"Who's there?" both of the women called.

CHAPTER FOUR

Caught!

"HELLO?" CALLED THE VOICE OF THE museum worker. "Who is that?"

I was busted. There was really no other option than to step out from behind the bookcase, which I did, while brushing the dust from my clothing and sneezing once more.

Beverly DeSantos took a few quick steps in my direction. "What did you hear?" she asked me.

"Nothing," I said. Truthfully, I hadn't overheard much. Or at least nothing I could understand without a little more context. "I was just . . . looking for the bathroom."

There was a pause as both women stared at me. Neither of them looked like they believed me. Who searches for the bathroom behind a dusty old bookcase?

It didn't seem to matter, though. Beverly turned back to Susan and said, "I hope you'll reconsider." Then she walked swiftly down the hallway and out through the STAFF ONLY door.

Susan let out a deep breath as soon as Beverly left the hallway. She looked incredibly relieved to no longer be speaking with her.

"You really can't be back here," she said while turning to face me. "The bathrooms are by the front desk. There are plenty of signs."

"Right," I said. "I'm sorry about that."

Susan began walking me toward the door. I didn't want to leave yet. Beverly and Susan had just had such a strange conversation, and I really wanted to ask Susan a few questions about it. I would have to get her to like me first, though.

"That other woman was pretty rude to you," I tried.

"Yes, well," said Susan. "She's always like that."

"Is she?" I asked.

Susan nodded. I didn't think she was going to say anything else, but then she continued, "She thinks she can tell me how to run my museum."

"Why would she think that?"

Susan looked at me suspiciously, as if I might be attempting to trick her. If I wanted to have a real conversation, I knew I'd have to give her a better reason to talk to me.

"The truth is, I'm a reporter," I said quickly. "That's why I was back here. I'm writing a story about the museum. I'm sorry about sneaking around like this, but I would love to talk to you, actually. It could be a great way to get the museum some more publicity."

Susan raised her eyebrows. She seemed as though she was considering it. Then she said, "More publicity?"

"Yes," I replied. "I work for a travel and lifestyle magazine. We encourage our readers to visit certain events around the country."

Susan looked around, as if someone might overhear us in the empty hallway. "If you're interested in writing about this curse business, I really can't talk about it. At least, not on the record. The police already suspect I'm wrapped up in it."

"That's okay," I said. "I can keep you anonymous."

"And this article—it won't be all about the curse, will it? You'll also encourage people to come see the photographs?"

"Definitely," I said. "Our readers would be very interested in an exhibit as great as this one."

This seemed to convince Susan somewhat. She was still frowning and looking at me with her brow creased, but she was also nodding.

"So what was going on with you and that woman?" I asked.

"I shouldn't even mention this," Susan said. "But that woman was Beverly DeSantos."

"Oh," I said. "Wow, really?" I tried my best to look surprised.

"That's right," said Susan. "Just because she donated

the photographs, she thinks she can tell me what to do with them."

"Because of the missing people?" I asked.

For a moment I was worried I had crossed a line and that Susan would stop talking to me. But luckily, she didn't seem to mind. She said, "Exactly. She thinks she should be able to decide what to do now."

I knew this next question was risky, but I had to ask. "The police seem to think you might be behind these disappearances, that you're trying to use the curse to stir up attention for the exhibit. Is there any truth to that?"

"No," said Susan sharply. "I might have pretended a photograph went missing and tried to blame it on the curse, but I wouldn't do that with a person."

"But you still haven't shut down the exhibit," I said. "Why not, if one of your employees has really gone missing? Grace Rogers—I read that was her name."

Susan crossed her arms over her chest. She seemed a little annoyed by the question, like maybe she had been asked this before. "I hardly even knew Grace

Rogers, and I don't believe she's actually gone *missing*," she said. "Grace had only worked here for a few weeks, and she'd practically begged me to hire her. Then she just skipped town, no notice, and right as we were getting more popular. Now I'm running this museum all on my own."

"But the image of her in one of the photographs," I said. "Where do you think it came from if you don't believe something happened to Grace? And why not take the exhibit down, especially after a second person has disappeared?"

"Someone's tampering with my exhibit," said Susan, clearly growing more annoyed with each of my questions. "I don't pretend to know why. And I haven't taken it down because, well, people have a right to see those photographs!"

She didn't seem entirely convinced by her own argument. "Oh, I agree," I said, hoping to calm her down and get her back on my side. "People should absolutely be able to see them. It's not as though you have anything to hide."

I wasn't sure that I really felt this way. Two missing people seemed like more than enough of a good reason to shut down the exhibit. But I also wanted Susan to continue talking to me, so I had to make her think I agreed with her.

Now that she seemed to believe I wasn't arguing with her, Susan's shoulders slumped. "Honestly," she said, lowering her voice, even though we were still alone, "the museum isn't doing very well. I thought we were going to have to close by the end of this year. But ever since Grace went missing, and now this other boy, well, we've never been so popular. I know the police are threatening to shut everything down in a few days, but if I took the exhibit down now, I'd have to close anyway. I might as well make some profit while I can. Does that sound just awful?"

I took a moment before answering. Really, I didn't think it sounded very good at all. I thought that Susan should be more worried about the missing people, especially since one of those people had been an employee of hers. I was still trying to think of something to say when it became clear that I had taken too long to respond and lost my chance to say anything at all. Susan took a step away from me and seemed to realize what she had just said.

"I'll take whatever publicity I can get for the museum," she said. "But remember that none of that was on the record." It was clear that we were done with our conversation.

"Of course," I said. "Thank you for speaking with me. I'll go now."

I walked quickly back to the STAFF ONLY door and turned the knob to exit, leaving Susan in the dusty hallway behind me.

I made my way outside the Carlisle Museum, and it looked as though the sun had finally managed to break through all that cloud cover. All the grass and the fall-colored trees outside were still flecked with drops of rainwater, but now everything was also sparkling in the new light.

I stood for a moment and studied the museum

building. It was large, made of the same red brick as most of the buildings in town. At first glance it looked impressive. But when I looked a little closer, I could see that one of the windows was actually cracking, the brick was badly damaged on the far left edge of the building, and the roof was missing its shingles in more than one section. Susan's admission that the museum wasn't doing well financially certainly explained the building's run-down condition.

"Nancy!" I heard someone calling me. "Over here!"

I looked to my right, and sitting on a bench in front of the museum were Bess, George, and a boy I didn't recognize. I was relieved to see my friends again. Even though I knew it hadn't actually been that long, I felt as though we had been separated for a while. I was also eager to tell them everything that had just happened.

"Hey," I said as I approached them. "Where did you guys go?"

"Sorry," said Bess. "It was just so crowded in there, we had to step outside."

I thought back to all the people inside and told

Bess that I completely understood. "I'm Nancy, by the way," I said to the boy sitting next to Bess and George.

"Right," said Bess. "Nancy, this is Lucas. He's here for the DeSantos exhibit as well."

I held my hand out to Lucas, and he said, "I was just telling Bess and George that I've been in town since the exhibit opened, about a week ago. So I'd be happy to show you guys around if you're interested."

Lucas had a nice, wide smile and large brown eyes. He was wearing a leather jacket, and a shark tooth hung on a chain around his neck. I also noticed that when he offered to show us around town, he looked at Bess specifically. That didn't surprise me: Bess usually had this effect on boys.

"Yeah," I said. "That would be great. Are you a fan of DeSantos, then?"

Lucas shrugged. "Not especially," he said. "I'm an art history student, specializing in historic photography. And I go to school a few hours from here."

"Oh, interesting," I said. "Are you a photographer too, then?"

Lucas laughed and said, "No, I'm a terrible photographer! I always loved the subject, though, so now I just study it."

"It must be an exciting thing to study," I said. "Do you—"

Before I could finish my thought, I happened to glance over at George. She was looking at me with wide eyes and was shaking one of her legs. I realized that she had been uncharacteristically quiet throughout this entire conversation, and I immediately became worried that something was wrong.

"George?" I asked. "Are you all right?"

George quickly looked around. Then, speaking in a voice that was both a whisper and a shout, she said, "We saw Beverly DeSantos!"

"*George,*" said Bess, glancing over at Lucas. Lucas looked between George and Bess, as if one of them might explain why seeing Beverly DeSantos was such a big deal. Neither of them did. "Is now the best time to talk about this?"

I knew what Bess meant. This conversation might

sound pretty strange to someone who had just met us.

George ignored her cousin and continued on anyway. "Beverly DeSantos stormed out of here just a few minutes ago," she said. "Right before you came out. She looked pretty upset."

"Well," I said, "there might be more to that story."

Bess and George both looked up at me. George had her brows furrowed, and Bess was tilting her head.

"What do you mean?" asked Bess.

"Yeah, and why are your clothes so dirty, Nancy?" asked George. They had clearly both just noticed that I was covered in dust.

"Um," I said. I wanted to tell them everything, but I felt strange explaining what had happened in front of someone I'd just met. I didn't know Lucas yet, and sometimes people can react a little strangely when you tell them you're an amateur detective. Especially since my story would involve me sneaking into a hallway that was off-limits and then lying about why I was there. Things may have gone well with Riley, but I didn't want to risk it twice in one day. Plus, I didn't want the whole town knowing I was there to investigate.

Luckily, Bess seemed to figure out exactly what I was thinking.

"Hey, Lucas," she said. "How about you give me that tour of the town? Nancy, you probably want to go back to the hotel and change."

George quickly picked up on what Bess was doing. "Actually," she said, "I wanted to grab something at the hotel too. So I'll go with Nancy."

"Great!" said Bess. "Lucas, is that all right with you?"

Lucas was smiling and nodding in Bess's direction. "Yeah," he said. "Sounds good."

"Then I'll meet you both at the hotel later today," said Bess, giving us a pointed look. "Ready, Lucas?"

Bess and Lucas stood up from the bench and began walking in the direction of downtown. They were talking animatedly, and even though I could no longer hear them, I could see that Bess was already making Lucas laugh. Just before they rounded the corner, Bess turned back to George and me to give us a quick wave. I knew she wanted to hear what had happened to me, but I was also grateful she'd managed to give George and me some time to talk privately.

I didn't really need to change my clothes. Most of the dust had just gotten on my coat. Now that the sun was out, it was easy enough to take off my jacket and shake off anything that was clinging to the fabric.

There was a steady stream of people entering and exiting the museum next to us, and I didn't want to be overheard. "Do you think there's anywhere more private around here?" I asked George.

"What about the park on the other side of the museum?" she suggested. "I saw a picnic table there that looks pretty secluded."

"That sounds perfect," I told her.

We headed over in the direction of the table. Now that it wasn't raining, it was much easier to look around and see that Shady Oaks was actually a really beautiful town. Almost everywhere there were large trees, most of the buildings were brick, and the walking path of this small park was lined with black metal lampposts to help guide the way. I could understand why a photographer would want to retire here and spend his final years taking photographs of the town.

The picnic table and benches were still dotted with rain, so George and I sat down on our jackets and began to talk.

"Tell me everything," said George.

I filled her in on the events of my recent adventure. The staff hallway, the argument between Beverly DeSantos and the museum curator, and what Susan had said to me afterward about Grace Rogers's disappearance and the subsequent increase in ticket sales.

"Wow," said George.

"I know," I said. "I'm not sure what to make of it yet."

George thought about everything I had told her for a minute. Eventually she said, "I'm pretty suspicious of Beverly DeSantos. Remember what Riley said, about that interview? Beverly didn't like her grandfather. So maybe she's trying to sabotage his exhibit now, and the argument you overheard was her trying to get Susan to help."

"Maybe," I said. "But then, why would Beverly even donate the photographs in the first place? Susan was also really happy about ticket sales, and she's already tried to fake this curse once. I don't think we can count her out as a suspect either."

Instead of responding, George waved at someone behind me. I turned around to see Riley heading toward us. Riley took long steps as she walked, so her movement was something between walking and skipping. As she made her way in our direction, her camera bumped against her from where it was still hanging around her neck. "Hey, George!" she called over to us. "Hey, Nancy!"

"Hi, Riley," I said, once she was closer. "How's it going?"

"Great!" Riley had a large smile on her face, and she looked eager to tell us something. "I have some good news."

George and I made brief eye contact before George turned back to Riley and asked, "Really? What is it?"

"After our conversation at the diner, I went back to

the hotel," she began. "And I was just about to head out again when I ran into Emily!"

Riley had her arms held out and she looked excited, like she had just told us a very important piece of information. But neither George nor I reacted much to it. I could tell by looking at George that, just like myself, she had no idea who Emily was.

"Emily?" asked George.

Riley nodded a little impatiently and then began to clarify. "Emily is the girlfriend of the second missing person!" she said. "The one who was crying in front of the museum this morning."

"Oh!" I said. "We wanted to talk to her."

"I figured," said Riley. "Anyway, she's staying at the same hotel we all are, and she said she'd be happy to answer some questions."

"Riley, that's incredible!" I said. "When can we see her?"

Riley beamed. "Now, if you want to."

George and I looked at each other and grinned. "We want to," I told Riley. "Let's go."

CHAPTER FIVE

The Unreliable Witness

GEORGE, RILEY, AND I MADE OUR WAY toward the Elder Root Inn. The clouds were patchy and occasionally rolling over the sun, which made everything warm and then cold and then back again.

The hotel wasn't a far walk, though I suspected most places within downtown Shady Oaks were in walking distance of one another. Next to me, George and Riley were looking at Riley's camera, and George was asking questions about why Riley still used film instead of digital.

George seemed genuinely interested in what Riley had to say, but I also knew that my friend would always end up on the side of new technology.

I was only half listening to their conversation. Instead I was thinking about what I'd ask Emily. Maybe her boyfriend had some connection to the museum like Grace did. I wondered if he knew Susan.

I was so wrapped up in my own thoughts that I barely realized when we reached our hotel. Like most of the buildings here, it was made of red brick. It was a thin building, and pretty tall, especially compared to most everything else there. Hanging out front was a small square sign that read ELDER ROOT INN in decorative gold cursive.

Inside, the lobby was covered in a deep-red carpet. There were mirrors and a few unusual sculptures lining the walls, and the front desk was just off to the right, next to a grouping of overstuffed chairs. It didn't look like we were going to have time to linger, though, since Riley rushed toward the staircase near the back of the hotel. George and I followed as

Riley dashed upstairs, taking two steps at a time.

"Hey, wait up!" called George. Riley was much taller than either of us and was having an easier time making it up the steep stairs quickly.

"Emily said she was in room 212," Riley called back, barely slowing down for us. "She said I could just stop by whenever."

We quickly reached the long, narrow hallway on the second floor. It was lined with carpet that matched the lobby, and the entire building seemed to be a little crooked, as if it were slanting to the right.

Riley scanned the room numbers, trying to find Emily's room. George turned toward me.

"Hey," she said in a low voice. "I'm a little worried Emily won't really want to talk to us."

"Why do you think that?"

"Her boyfriend is missing," George said. "Would you want to talk about that with an amateur detective? She might be upset and just want to be left alone."

I considered this for a moment. George was probably right, but I felt confident I could make Emily comfortable enough to answer a few questions. "We'll just be really polite," I said.

George laughed. "That has worked in the past."

Just then Riley stopped in front of a door a little ways down from where George and I were standing.

"Hey, guys!" Riley called while waving us over. "This is 212."

George and I jogged over to where Riley was standing and waited as she knocked on the door. For a moment, it didn't sound like there was anyone inside. But then we heard the sound of someone approaching the door, and watched as Emily quickly opened it all the way.

"Hey, Riley!" she said, smiling at us. "And you must be Nancy, right? The detective?"

"Well," I said, "amateur detective."

"Right!" she said. "Please come in, come in."

Emily stepped off to the side and gestured in toward her room. I looked back at George before stepping inside. I could see that we were both completely shocked by the way Emily was acting. She seemed perfectly fine. She even seemed happy to see us. I knew that people often deal with stress in different ways, but I still couldn't help but be taken by surprise.

"Excuse the mess," she said, clearing a place for us to sit down on the bed and in the few chairs the room had. Emily's room was a little messy, mainly just dirty clothes lying around, but I didn't really mind. I took one of the chairs, with a yellow sweater still thrown across the back, and George took the other. Riley leaned up against the windowsill behind us.

"No, I understand," I said. "You've been dealing with a lot recently."

Emily let out a huff as she sat on the bed with a bounce and said, "That's true. Riley said you're trying to figure out what happened to Jacob?"

"That's Emily's boyfriend," supplied Riley.

"We are," I said. "We originally came to Shady Oaks because I'd heard about the missing museum employee, Grace Rogers. But now there's your boyfriend, Jacob, as well."

Emily nodded. "And the police aren't doing anything," she said.

"Really?" asked George. "I thought they were threatening to shut down the museum."

"And they brought you and Susan in for questioning," I added.

"Well, yes," said Emily. "They did. But I don't understand why they won't just close the exhibit now. Really, I think they just want to ignore it, because the exhibit is bringing in so much money for the town. If they found something and had to shut it down, everyone would be really upset."

"I was told that the police believe Susan is behind all this," I said. "They're hoping she'll come forward before the end of the week."

Emily let out a sound that was halfway between a snort and a laugh. "Susan isn't going to come forward," she said.

"Why do you think that?" I asked.

"Because she isn't responsible for the missing people," said Emily. "No one in town is. Those photographs are cursed, and as long as the museum is open, people are just going to keep going missing."

Off to my right I saw George roll her eyes, but I didn't want Emily to get offended and think that we didn't believe her. I figured that the best thing to do would be to get as much information as I could from her, even if she might have a different interpretation of everything than I would.

"Emily," I said, "why don't you tell us everything, from the beginning?"

Emily nodded and told us how she and Jacob had visited the exhibit last night. The museum was just about to close, and they were the last two people there. She was looking at a photograph, and when she eventually turned around, Jacob was gone.

"I tried to call him, but his phone was dead. Not like there's service here anyway. But I assumed he had just gone back to the hotel to charge it," she said. "So I came back here too. But he never showed. Then I went to the museum this morning and, well, you saw, right? I suppose Jacob isn't missing, though, because I know exactly where he is. He's trapped in one of DeSantos's photographs."

"And you believe in the curse," I clarified. I wanted to make sure I understood her perfectly. "You think that Terry Lawrence cursed his old partner's photographs so no one would display them again. Why do you think Lawrence was capable of doing that?"

Emily shrugged. "He said he could, in interviews. Christopher DeSantos wasn't a good person. He got his fame by using other people. And now people are literally being taken into his photographs."

"He used people?" I asked. "Do you mean he used Lawrence?"

"Yes," said Emily. "DeSantos took the credit for a photograph actually taken by Terry Lawrence, so Lawrence cursed him and his work. It's what he deserved."

"Right," I said. I wasn't sure what to make of Emily's theory, or of Emily herself. I knew I needed more information from a different source. I was about to end the interview, but Riley beat me to it.

"Christopher DeSantos didn't steal credit from anyone. No one really knows who took that photograph. And his photographs definitely aren't cursed. Why come to Shady Oaks for this exhibit if you don't even like DeSantos?" Riley's arms were crossed over her chest and she was looking at Emily distrustfully.

Throughout the conversation with Emily, I had forgotten that Riley was such a big Christopher DeSantos fan. Of course she wouldn't agree with Emily's theories.

I didn't want the two of them to argue over this, but Riley had actually asked a good question. Why *was* Emily here?

I turned to Emily and waited for her answer. Her mouth was open and she appeared to be searching for something to say. "Because of Jacob," she said finally. "That's also how I know so much about the curse. Jacob talked about it all the time. He believed in it and he wanted to visit Shady Oaks to see if anything might go wrong at the exhibit. He didn't expect to disappear himself. The curse is only meant to affect anyone who tries to display the photographs. He just wanted to look at them."

"And did you always believe in the curse?" I asked.

Emily shook her head. "Not until Jacob went missing," she said. "But now I have to believe, don't I? And clearly the curse affects anyone who interacts with the display too. I'm not going to stop telling people the real story. Not until the police shut down that exhibit for good and hopefully release Jacob from the curse."

I could sense Riley shifting behind me, and I didn't want her to say anything else to upset Emily. "Thank you so much for answering our questions," I said quickly. "Maybe I could stop by again? If anything else comes up."

"That would be fine," Emily said. She was watching Riley, though, and she was definitely acting much colder than when we had first arrived. I hoped she would still be willing to answer questions, if I needed to ask her anything in the future.

"Great," I said. "George. Riley."

I nodded toward the door, and the three of us stood

and filed outside. Just before I shut the door behind us, I turned to wave at Emily and said, "Thanks again."

Emily responded with only a slight smile that didn't quite look genuine.

We made our way down through the lobby and back outside, where Riley quickly turned to me and said, "Sorry about that, Nancy. But you don't really believe any of that, do you? DeSantos didn't use Terry Lawrence. If anything, it was the other way around."

Truthfully, I wasn't sure what to believe. I knew there was no such thing as curses, but as far as the relationship between the two photography partners, I just didn't have enough information.

"Why do you think it was the other way around?" asked George.

"DeSantos was much more talented than Lawrence," said Riley. "Everyone knew it. Lawrence was jealous of DeSantos long before they had their falling-out."

"How do you know all this?" I asked.

"There are plenty of interviews and articles from

that time. I could send you some resources if you want."

"That would be great," I said.

"And anyway," continued Riley, "DeSantos was just as hurt by the ending of their friendship as Lawrence was. People were so focused on the gossip that they stopped giving DeSantos the artistic credit he really deserved."

"Thanks, Riley," I said. "For telling us this and for finding Emily in the first place. You've helped a lot."

Riley nodded and then told us she was going to hang out at the hotel for a bit, before finally heading over for another look at the exhibit. George and I waved at her as she disappeared inside.

"Well, talking to Emily sure was a dead end," said George as soon as Riley was gone.

"What do you mean?" I asked.

"Cursed photographs? Don't tell me you're buying any of that, Nancy."

"Of course not," I said. "But I don't think talking to Emily was a waste of time. Don't you think it's strange how eager she was to talk to us or how long it took her to come up with an explanation for being in town? I think there's something going on with her."

"It's possible," said George. "But how do we find out for sure? Do you have any more leads to follow?"

I didn't. I shook my head at George before looking up and down the street. There were plenty of small businesses around, and people walking nearby who might have been locals or maybe some more DeSantos fans.

"Let's explore the town," I said to George. "We'll talk to as many people as possible. Someone will *have* to know something."

Bess had left a note at the front desk of the hotel saying she and Lucas were still exploring the town and she would meet us at the hotel for dinner that evening. So George and I spent the rest of the day walking into every store and local office we could. Everyone seemed more than happy to point us in the direction of the museum or to answer our questions about the exhibit, but as soon as we mentioned the missing people, they suddenly had nothing more to say. Everyone seemed more closed off whenever we mentioned Beverly DeSantos especially, as if they did not like her, and I was beginning to understand how much of an outcast she was in this town.

Eventually, when it was starting to grow dark, we trudged back to the hotel. George was complaining about the pain her feet were in, and how tired she was, and how hungry she was, and I couldn't say I disagreed. We'd been on our feet all day and had spoken to so many people that it was discouraging to head back to the hotel without any new leads or clues. It had also continued to rain off and on all day, and now George and I were both slightly damp and shivering from the cold.

We entered our hotel room to find the lights already on. "Hey, Bess!" I said as I stepped inside.

Bess was sitting on one of the beds with her legs delicately crossed. She had a pizza sitting next to her, and the smell of it was filling the entire room.

"Hey, guys!" she said. "I thought you might be hungry."

"You thought right," said George, collapsing onto the bed opposite Bess and grabbing a slice of pizza. "Thank you," she mumbled after taking her first bite.

Bess didn't wait a minute before she turned to me and said, "So what happened to you in the museum today?"

"Oh, right!" I said. I had forgotten how long it had been since I'd seen Bess. She didn't even know about what had happened in the staff hallway between Beverly DeSantos and Susan yet. I quickly filled her in, and told her about our strange conversation with Emily. "George and I went around town after that to ask everyone some questions. But no one wanted to talk to us."

"Why not?" asked Bess.

"I'm not sure," I said. "Some people seemed a bit uncomfortable, especially when I brought up Beverly DeSantos. I wouldn't be surprised if some of them believe she's behind all this, and that she's the one kidnapping people."

"Well," said Bess, "I might have some more information about her. Do you remember that interview Riley told us about?"

"The one where Beverly said she wished she had been born into a different family?" I asked.

"Exactly!" said Bess. "Well, Lucas told me that it was actually a really big deal when it came out. Beverly was only eighteen when she gave it, but Christopher DeSantos's fans were all really upset. They've hated her ever since. Maybe she's kidnapping her grandfather's fans in order to destroy his latest exhibit. I mean, it would be pretty extreme, but apparently she has a major grudge against everyone involved."

George reached forward for another piece of pizza and said, "It's seeming more and more like Beverly. Don't you think, Nancy?"

"Hmm," I said. "I don't know. She sounded really upset about the missing people when I overheard her in the hallway. I still have so many questions."

"Like what?" asked George.

"Like, if this is Beverly," I said, "how is she getting

the images of the missing people into those photo-graphs? Wouldn't she need the combination to open up the picture frames? And if she did kidnap Grace and Jacob, then where is she hiding them now? No one we spoke to today saw either of them leave the museum. And what is the end goal here? Is it all just to make sure no one has another DeSantos exhibit again?"

The three of just looked at one another. None of us had the answers.

"So what do we do next?" asked Bess, breaking the silence.

"Riley said she would e-mail us more information about Christopher DeSantos and his work partner, Terry Lawrence," I said. "I feel like there's something I'm missing in their story. I want to read through that information as soon as possible."

"Too bad there's no Wi-Fi in this hotel," George grumbled. "Or good cell service anywhere around here."

"Oh!" said Bess. "Lucas and I went to a coffee shop today. They have free Wi-Fi for customers. I can take us there tomorrow morning."

"Perfect!" I said. I looked over to see George nodding enthusiastically. I suspected she was less excited about reading more on the subject of Christopher DeSantos and Terry Lawrence than she was just to get back onto the Internet in general.

CHAPTER SIX

Coffee, Croissants, and Curses

THE NEXT MORNING BESS, GEORGE, AND I headed over to the coffee shop Bess had mentioned. It was called the Bean and Briar Coffee Shop, and it felt more like an overfilled living room than a café. Instead of regular tables and chairs, there was an assortment of large, plushy sofas and coffee tables. We found a pair of couches, one large and one small, near the window. When we sat down, we all sank into them, and I knew it was going to be difficult to stand back up.

We also ordered some pastries for breakfast, and three cups of coffee. George pulled out her laptop and had it propped up on her knees. She was typing furiously.

"Did Riley send us anything?" I asked her, as I cautiously sipped my hot, steaming beverage.

George nodded from behind her screen. "Apparently she went to the library earlier this morning to do some more research and send us the resources. I think she's caught the detective bug, Nancy."

I laughed. "Well, that's lucky for us."

George spun the computer around so Bess and I could see the screen. There was a photograph pulled up of two men posing near a large canyon. I didn't recognize one of them, but the other was clearly a young Christopher DeSantos. He looked younger than any image I had seen of him so far, like he was maybe in his twenties. I guessed that the man next to him had to be Terry Lawrence.

Both of the men were smiling, and they had their arms around each other. They were dressed in boots and cargo shorts, and looking more closely, I could see that they each were wearing an assortment of trinkets: bracelets and necklaces and other things they must have picked up on their travels. Terry Lawrence even had a large, triangle-shaped earring hanging from his right ear.

"Could you send this to my phone, George?" I asked. I wanted to download it now, while we still had Wi-Fi. "And any other photographs you find."

George nodded. She also showed us the photograph that had supposedly ended DeSantos and Lawrence's partnership. It was a beautiful image, a shot of a canyon angled in such a way that the formation seemed to go on forever. But truthfully, I still liked the photographs I had seen of people more. Like the one of DeSantos and Lawrence. I felt like there had to be more clues inside that photograph that I just wasn't seeing yet.

"Anything else, George?" I asked.

"I found Terry Lawrence's obituary," said George. "If that helps."

"What does it say?" asked Bess.

"Not too much," said George. "It says that he continued taking photographs for most of his life, until he eventually lost his sight. He moved to West Virginia to be closer to his children and his three grandchildren and died in 2010. That's all, really."

I leaned back into the soft sofa. None of this was as clear a lead as I was hoping for. Bess, George, and I all went quiet for a few moments. George started typing away on her laptop again, brow scrunched as she sorted through information. Bess and I went back to our pastries and coffee, both of us trying to work through the mystery.

After a while, I noticed that someone was talking fairly loudly on the other side of the coffee shop. I sat up and looked behind me. There was a small crowd of people gathered on that side of the shop. Some of the people were sitting and some were standing. They were all looking toward someone in the middle of the group, and when the crowd shifted, I could see who was in the middle of it all: Emily.

"What's wrong, Nancy?" asked Bess, who must

have noticed me changing my position to see what was going on.

"One second," I whispered back. I wanted to hear what Emily was saying, and I didn't want her to see or hear us just yet.

It was difficult to fully understand her, but it sounded as though Emily was retelling the story of Jacob's disappearance. I heard her once more insist that the photographs in the exhibit were cursed. I watched the expressions of the people in the crowd. Some of them seemed skeptical, but others were nodding along with everything Emily said.

"We should all call the police," Emily said. "We should demand that they shut down the museum now, before anyone else goes missing."

This idea was met with mixed replies. Some of the crowd seemed to agree with her, but others were shaking their heads. If the town really was benefitting from all the increased tourism, I knew Emily was going to have a difficult time convincing everyone that the museum should close.

I turned back to Bess and gestured in the direction of the crowd. "That's Emily," I said. "The girl Riley, George, and I talked to yesterday."

Bess peered over the edge of the couch. "If I didn't know any better," she said, "I'd say she was enjoying telling her story."

"I was thinking the same thing," I said. I still wasn't sure what to make of Emily, but there was definitely some piece of information about her that I was missing. I decided to try and interview her again later in the day to see what I could learn.

Just then Bess reached down for her phone. "It's Lucas," she said, while clearly reading a text. "Do you mind if I invite him over here for breakfast?"

"I don't know, Bess," I said. Really, I wanted to keep discussing the case, and I wasn't sure that was going to be possible with someone else around. "Do you think we can trust him with all this information?"

"Nancy," said Bess, "Lucas is just a student! He isn't even from around here. Besides, he might be able to give us some insight on this case. I'm sure he knows more about Christopher DeSantos and Terry Lawrence than we'll be able to find on our own."

"That's a good point," I said. Telling Riley about the case had turned out to be the best move we'd made. Why not bring some more expertise in? "All right, invite him. Let's just all be careful with what we say."

Bess nodded and quickly texted Lucas back. George gave me a thumbs-up over her computer screen, confirming that she knew to speak carefully while Lucas was around. After only a few minutes, Lucas entered the coffee shop. He was wearing nearly the same thing as yesterday, which was his leather jacket and jeans and his shark-tooth necklace. Once he spotted us, he waved and headed over in our direction.

"Have you guys been listening to that?" he said as he sat down. He gestured over to where Emily was telling her story.

"Nancy was," said Bess. "She thinks something suspicious is going on."

"Bess," I said. That was exactly the kind of information I was nervous about sharing with Lucas.

"Really?" said Lucas. "So you are here to try and solve the case of the missing people, then."

Bess and I quickly looked at Lucas. Even George looked up from behind her computer screen. I turned to Bess, thinking she must have mentioned something to Lucas about me being an amateur detective.

Bess understood what I was thinking almost immediately. She said, "I didn't say anything, Nancy. Really."

"She didn't," said Lucas. "Actually . . ." He paused here and looked like he was possibly embarrassed, or maybe just nervous. "I've heard about you before. You're Nancy Drew, right? I've read about some of the mysteries you've solved. You're pretty impressive."

"Oh," I said. "Thank you." I was completely surprised that Lucas had heard of me before. I'd be lying if I said I wasn't a little bit flattered, too. I looked at Bess and she was beaming at me. She was clearly pleased that Lucas was making such a good impression.

Bess, Lucas, and I continued talking a little more about Emily's story and, eventually, about Lucas's studies as well. I was trying to keep my guard up, but it appeared that Bess was right about Lucas. He did seem very nice.

Finally George announced that she'd found Beverly DeSantos's interview. "Should I give you the highlights?" she asked.

I nodded enthusiastically. "Just keep your voice down," I said.

George began skimming through the interview and gave the rest of us a summary. Mainly it said that Beverly didn't enjoy growing up in the public eye. "According to the article," said George, "Beverly said that she really didn't like how many photographs of her as a child ended up being sold to complete strangers who just wanted to own an original DeSantos. Some of them even ended up in magazines, or published in other places. She did say that she wished she had been born into another family. The writer of the article wrote that Beverly looked sullen as she said this, bordering on angry."

"I don't know, Nancy," said Bess. "That doesn't sound very good."

"Yeah," said George. "If we're looking for a motive, this could definitely be it."

"Maybe," I said. There was something about it that didn't sit right with me, and I couldn't help but think that there was certainly a difference between hating your grandfather and not wanting to be famous.

"What do you think, Lucas?" asked Bess, turning toward him.

"Oh," said Lucas. He was shifting in his seat. "I'm not sure. I mean, I'm not a detective."

"But you have to admit it's not a positive portrayal," said George.

"Well," said Lucas. "Yes, I can admit that. And I do know that when it came out, it made a lot of DeSantos fans pretty mad. I'm not sure his strongest supporters ever got over it. Some of them can get pretty fanatical about this stuff."

I thought about this for a moment. Lucas was making a good point. What if a DeSantos fan was doing all this to frame Beverly, to get back at her for her negative interview? It was certainly possible and seemed just as likely as Beverly herself being a suspect.

Regardless, I still didn't have enough information. "I think we need to change direction," I said. "There are other questions we can answer. Like, how are those missing people showing up in DeSantos's photographs at all? And where are Grace and Jacob now?"

Lucas shook his head. He said, "I've been here since the exhibit opened. When Grace disappeared, no one saw her leave the museum. It was like she just vanished. And the same thing with Jacob. Not one person saw him leave the building."

"Well," I said, "just because no one saw them leave the museum doesn't mean they vanished. Or . . . maybe they didn't leave at all."

Lucas was clearly confused by this, but after a moment Bess and George seemed to know what I meant.

"Oh!" said Bess. "That door behind the bookshelf!"

"You think they've been trapped back there?" asked George.

"I think it's possible," I said. I turned to Lucas and quickly told him the story of my run-in with Beverly DeSantos and Susan in the museum's staff hallway. "The museum looks so large from the outside," I said, "but the exhibit space is relatively small. There has to be more than enough space to keep two people hidden back there. I want to try and get through that door again. Maybe I can figure out the combination for the keypad over the door handle, or maybe the combination is written down somewhere, in one of the offices in that hallway. Honestly, I'm not sure what to make of Christopher DeSantos and his relationship with Terry Lawrence, or his relationship to his granddaughter. But that doorway has to be something."

Bess and George both nodded at me. "So back to the museum?" asked George. She began typing faster as she spoke, and I knew she was trying to get in as much Wi-Fi time as possible.

"Back to the museum," I confirmed.

"Lucas," said Bess, "do you want to come with us?"

"Um." Lucas paused. "Actually, I just remembered

I already made plans with a friend. Maybe I'll see you guys later. Bye, Bess."

Lucas quickly stood, threw his leather jacket back on, and headed toward the door. I looked at Bess, and she seemed a little surprised by his sudden departure. I couldn't say I felt the same way, though. I couldn't help but wonder if inviting someone to sneak around the restricted section of a museum was just too much for a new friendship.

CHAPTER SEVEN

A Warning

BESS, GEORGE, AND I BEGAN WALKING IN the direction of the museum. It was another day of confusing weather in Shady Oaks. One minute it was overcast and on the verge of pouring down rain. The next minute the sun was peeking through the clouds and catching on all the fall leaves and it was nearly a warm day. I kept my red raincoat on just in case. Underneath my raincoat, however, all I needed was a long-sleeved T-shirt to feel perfectly comfortable.

Just like yesterday, the museum seemed to be filled with people. Even as we stood outside and watched how many people walked in and out the front door, I could tell it was going to be difficult to sneak around unnoticed.

As the three of us began walking up the museum's front steps, I leaned in close to Bess and George. "It'll be easier for just one of us to get into that hallway than all of us," I said. "I think I'll need you both to create a distraction. And I'll try to get through the STAFF ONLY door while everyone is looking at the two of you. Is that all right?"

"Sure," said Bess. "But what kind of distraction?"

I thought about this as we walked into the exhibit room, but as it turned out, I wouldn't need a distraction at all. Everyone inside was gathered around one photograph on the far side of the space. They were all pushing against one another, and no one was looking in the direction of the staff hallway at all.

"Actually," I said, "that'll work. I'll be right back. You guys check out what everyone is looking at. I hope it's not another missing person."

Bess and George nodded at me and then began to

walk over to where everyone else was standing. I hung back and made my way slowly toward the STAFF ONLY door. Doing my best to look unsuspicious, I leaned against the wall next to the restricted door. When I was certain no one was looking, I opened the door just a crack and slipped inside.

The hallway looked just the same as I remembered it. There was still all the clutter and the dust, and as soon as I stepped inside, I sneezed twice in quick succession.

First I wanted to check the door behind the bookcase and make sure it was still locked. I walked as fast as I could manage while still being as quiet as possible. It took me only a few light steps, walking on the balls of my feet, to reach the end of the hallway and slip behind the large bookcase. I reached my arm out toward the door handle and gave it a tug downward. Still locked. Above the door's keypad there were four small lights. They weren't on now, but I was willing to bet this meant the combination would be four numbers long. I just had to figure out what they were.

I stepped out from behind the shelf and dusted

myself off. I remembered seeing two offices in this hallway. I thought that maybe one of them had the code for the door written down somewhere.

In the first office there was a desk, but otherwise the room was mainly empty. I walked around anyway, just to make sure I wasn't missing anything. There were frames that looked similar to those out in the hallway, and leaning against one of the walls was a collection of large signs. But there really wasn't anything that made me think this room was still being used as an active office space. I walked back over to the door and took one last look before moving on.

The second office was a bit larger, and slightly less cluttered than everywhere else. There was a name tag on the desk that read SUSAN MILLER, and behind that was a large pile of paperwork and mail. I began shuffling through it all, and found that Susan had a number of unpaid bills and overdue payment notices. She clearly had not been lying about the museum not doing very well.

Unlike the rest of the room, Susan's desk was pretty well organized, so I was able to search through everything fairly quickly. I opened one of her drawers to find an old card she'd received, the lease for the museum, and letters from a few more companies the museum owed money to. I got out my phone and took photographs of them all, in case they might be useful in the future.

I'd already been back here for a while, and I knew that the longer I stayed, the more likely it would become that I would get caught. Reluctantly, I gave up the search and crept back over to the bookcase.

If Susan had chosen a random set of numbers to be her combination, then I had no hope of figuring it out. But most people don't use random numbers. I had a few ideas for what the combination could be. First I tried the museum's address, which I had just found written down in Susan's office. It didn't work. I tried the year the museum had opened, and the last four digits of the museum's phone number. Frustratingly, the door remained locked. Whatever Susan had chosen as her combination, it wasn't written down in her office.

As a last resort, I tried just knocking on the door. If Grace and Jacob were trapped back there, maybe they would hear my knock and know that someone was searching for them. After knocking a few times, I pressed my ear to the door and listened. It was completely silent.

I let out a deep breath. I had been so certain that I'd be able to get through this door, and if I couldn't find a way inside, I really wasn't sure what to do next. I decided to check Susan's office one last time and was just about to walk back out from behind the bookcase when I heard a voice say, "Now, *really*."

I stopped moving. Whoever was in the hallway couldn't see me yet, but I must have been making a great deal of noise as I typed codes into the door's keypad and tried to force the door open again and again. Not to mention the knocking.

"Yes, I heard you," said the voice. "You can come out now."

I could recognize the voice now. It was clearly Susan's wheezing, nervous way of speaking. Reluctantly, I made my way out from behind the bookcase and turned to see her standing in the hallway with her arms crossed over her chest.

Right as I stepped out, I noticed that Susan had been watching the bookcase with her eyes narrowed and her expression stern. But as soon as she saw that it was me, her expression turned to one of complete shock.

I wasn't sure what to make of the way Susan was looking at me. All I knew was that I desperately wanted to get behind that door.

"Oh, you're here?" Susan asked me. I thought it was a strange way to phrase that question. Even more strange, however, was the way Susan was looking at me. She was staring at me like she was perhaps a bit frightened. I nearly questioned her about this, but instead I decided that getting behind that door had to be my first priority.

"I know," I said. "I'm sorry, I shouldn't be back here. But I really need you to open this door. I think the missing people from the photographs, Grace and Jacob, are trapped in whatever space is back there."

I knew it was a long shot that Susan would believe me. I also knew it was even possible that Susan *knew* the missing people might be back there, but things were going so well for her business she just didn't want to look into it. I didn't have a better idea, though, and I knew I had to try something.

Susan took a moment to respond. She still looked surprised to see me back here. But then she seemed to come back to her senses and to fully process what I had just said.

Looking a bit frustrated with me, she said, "There is no one trapped back there. It's just a closed-off wing of the museum! And it's only closed because we don't have the funds to keep such a large space running. What kind of an article are you writing?"

I ignored Susan's question. "But isn't it possible that someone could have gotten back there when you weren't watching?" I asked. "You're the only one running this entire museum. You must be very busy."

"No," said Susan. She seemed very certain about this. "That door is always locked and no one has access. And look." She pointed up at the ceiling. In the corner of the hallway was a small video camera with a blinking red light. "We have a security camera here and three in the exhibit space. I would have seen if anyone was sneaking around. And before you ask: No, you can't see the video camera's footage. The police have already viewed it and they didn't find anything. You can't think you'd do better than the *police*."

I couldn't believe I hadn't noticed the video camera. Arguing with her about seeing the footage seemed futile. But there was something else Susan had said that didn't sit right with me.

"There really isn't anyone who has access?" I asked her. "I mean, obviously you must."

Susan rolled her eyes. "Well, of course I do. It's the same combination as the front door to the museum, so my employees and I all know the code. Well, employee. Grace was my only one. And, well . . ." Susan paused here and seemed reluctant to keep speaking. "Beverly DeSantos has access too."

I could feel my blood run cold. "Beverly DeSantos has access to this door? Why?"

Susan let out a huff of breath. "It was in Beverly's

contract when she donated the photographs to the museum." Susan seemed very unhappy about this. "She wanted to be able to come visit the collection in private, at night, whenever she wanted. But I don't see why you need any of this information for your article."

"Every detail helps," I said. If Beverly was one of the few people who knew the combination to this door, then it was looking more and more likely that she had something to do with all this. Especially if she had specifically asked to be able to visit the museum privately, at night. I was about to try and ask Susan to open the door one last time, when she told me it was time to leave.

Susan ushered me over to the door back into the DeSantos exhibit and held it open for me.

"I'm glad you're writing about the exhibit, and I'm really not in any position to turn down free publicity. But please do not try to get into this hallway again," she warned me as I stepped back through the doorway. Susan pointed toward the far end of the exhibit, where a crowd of people was still gathered. "I'm not sure what you're trying to do here, or what you've gotten yourself involved in. But in my opinion, you should be much more careful."

"What do you mean?" I asked her. But she had disappeared back into the staff hallway and closed the door.

I did a quick survey of the exhibit space, focusing specifically on the ceiling. Just like Susan had said, there were three cameras dotting the room. I approached the closest one and looked up at it. It looked identical to the one in the staff hallway, and it too had a steadily blinking red light. Susan had said there wasn't anything suspicious in the video cameras' footage, but I wasn't sure that I believed her. There was something strange about the video camera itself, though I wasn't sure what it was exactly.

Eventually I spotted Bess and George standing near the crowd of people, and I made my way over to them.

"No luck," I said. "I couldn't figure out the combination."

Bess and George turned around to face me, and to my surprise they both looked incredibly worried.

George had her brows drawn together, and Bess was fiddling with the ends of her hair.

"Nancy!" said Bess. "Thank God you're back."

"What?" I said. "Why do you say that?"

Instead of answering, George just grabbed my hand and began dragging me farther into the crowd of people. "There's something you need to see," she said, sounding very serious.

As George and I began making our way through the crowd, I noticed that everyone was turning back to look at me. As soon as they each saw my face, they either pulled away from me, or else leaned over to their neighbor and began pointing at me and whispering.

"George?" I asked. "What's going on?"

We were at the front of the crowd, and I could finally see what everyone had been looking at. It was another photograph of Shady Oaks in the 1940s, but it wasn't the one that contained the image of Grace or the one with Jacob. There was someone new trapped within the frozen world of a DeSantos photograph. Me.

CHAPTER EIGHT

~❧~

Overexposure

GEORGE AND BESS WERE STANDING JUST behind me as I stared at my own face, impossibly walking through the background of an old photograph.

"Is that *me*?" I asked, even though it clearly was. "How is that possible?"

Bess was next to me and shaking her head.

"That's what we were asking," said George. "And you clearly aren't missing. You're standing right here."

I looked more closely at the photograph. It looked similar to the images of Grace and Jacob. The image of me matched the texture and tone of the rest of the photograph, and it was once more a full-body image that made it appear as though I was walking through the background of a Shady Oaks of the past.

Unlike the images of Grace and Jacob, however, there were a few more details I could notice in my own picture. In the photograph, I was wearing my raincoat. At first I assumed the picture of me must have been taken today. But then I noticed my cable-knit sweater, only just visible beneath my jacket. So the image must have been taken yesterday.

There was also, I noticed, a strange line running down my torso. It was fuzzy and I couldn't tell what it was, but it looked like maybe something had gotten between myself and the camera lens.

"Nancy?" asked Bess. "What does this mean?"

We were still surrounded by people, and they were all still looking in my direction. So I nodded in the direction of the museum's front door, and the three of us headed outside.

We stepped out the door, and it was now fully cloudy. It had also started to rain a little, and George and I pulled our jacket hoods up over our heads. Bess pulled out her polka-dotted umbrella and held it over the three of us. We were standing just to the side of the museum, but with the rain, I felt confident no one was going to hang around and listen in on our conversation.

"I think the photograph is a warning," I said. "Whoever is behind all this has to be improvising now. I think whoever kidnapped Grace and Jacob wants me to stop investigating. Or I'm going to be next."

"That sounds really bad," said Bess. "Do we stop investigating?" Both she and George looked concerned by the idea that I might be the next target, and I could tell that Bess in particular was remembering being kidnapped herself, not too long ago.

"Actually," I said, "this might be a good thing."

George's eyebrows shot up and Bess's eyes widened. "Nancy," said George. "How is this *possibly* a good thing?"

"The only reason someone would send us a warning was if we were on the right track," I explained. "I still think I'm right about that door in the museum.

And now I know how to get back there. I just have to ask someone for the door code."

"Ask who?" asked Bess. "Who knows it besides Susan?"

I smiled. "Beverly DeSantos."

Bess, George, and I began walking downtown, in the direction of the diner and the Bean and Briar Coffee Shop and all the other stores we had walked by while in Shady Oaks. As we walked, my friends tried to convince me that talking to Beverly DeSantos was a bad idea.

"Don't you think Beverly DeSantos is behind all this?" asked George.

"Yeah," said Bess. "I thought she was our number one suspect."

I shook my head. "I just have a hunch that it isn't her," I said. "Why would she donate all those photographs to the exhibit just to sabotage the museum later? Plus, I'm beginning to think that the interview Beverly did got blown way out of proportion. I don't think she really meant that she hated her family. I'm thinking she just didn't want to be famous."

"But do we have evidence for any of that?" asked George. "It sounds like you're just guessing."

I stopped walking. George was right; I was mainly just speculating about all of this. That wasn't how I preferred to solve mysteries. Normally, I would want to find a lot more evidence before jumping to conclusions. But I had a gut feeling about Beverly, and I felt like I should trust it.

"I am guessing," I said. "But regardless, Susan is never going to tell us the combination. The police think this is all a publicity stunt, and Susan said that they already went through her security footage and didn't find anything. Grace was the museum's only employee, and she's missing. The only other person who knows the combination is Beverly DeSantos. So I have to ask her."

Bess and George both looked at me and eventually agreed. I could tell that they were skeptical about this plan. But luckily for me, they were also great friends who were willing to trust me and my ideas, even the ones that made them both nervous.

"All right," said Bess. "So how do we find Beverly DeSantos?"

That was a good question. I had no idea where Beverly lived. But Shady Oaks was so small, and Beverly was such a local celebrity, that I felt confident most people living here must know. The only question was whether they would be willing to tell us.

"By asking around," I said. "We'll ask anyone from Shady Oaks that we come across. Let's start with shop owners and employees." I gestured toward the row of shops and stores ahead of us, and Bess and George nodded.

We started with the Bean and Briar Coffee Shop, followed by the local grocery store, a pet store, and the post office. We didn't have much luck. Once we began asking about Beverly, no one seemed to want to speak to us.

The owner of the local grocery store, wearing a heavy white apron around his stomach, even said that he wouldn't tell us anything because he didn't want to be the next person to disappear.

"Do you really believe Beverly DeSantos is kidnapping people, though?" George asked him.

"Yes," said the man seriously, before ushering us out of his store.

After we were back outside, George turned to Bess and me and said, "I think everyone in this town is terrified of Beverly DeSantos."

"It sure seems like it," said Bess.

"Yeah," I agreed. "But let's keep going. All we need is one person who is willing to talk to us. C'mon, let's try this place next."

We walked up to the arts and crafts store I had noticed when we first got into town, the one with a large portrait of Christopher DeSantos in the front window display. It was one of those places that allows you to make your own ceramic mugs and plates and then decorate them yourself.

The door chimed as we stepped inside. It was a small shop, and up at the front was an even smaller lady. She was an older woman, with gray hair brushed up into a loose bun, and looked as though she was barely five feet tall. She was wearing large, round glasses and was peering up at us from behind the front counter. "Welcome," she said, smiling at us kindly.

We smiled and waved at her. "I'll go talk to her," Bess whispered to us. Bess was excellent at charming people, and I hoped this woman would be no exception.

George and I spent a few minutes silently looking around the shop. The shelves were lined with mugs, bowls, plates, and other dishware. Some of them were hand-painted in all kinds of colorful hues, while others were decorated with photos of babies and smiling family portraits. Lining one of the walls was a series of plates featuring photographs of the same two dogs. They were both mastiffs and they looked incredibly large.

"Those are my dogs," said a voice behind us. I turned around to see Bess and the older woman. The woman was gesturing toward the plates. "I made those myself. Do you like them?"

I nodded enthusiastically, even though I thought

they were maybe a little odd. "They're great," I said.

George was standing next to me and had yet to answer the question. I quickly elbowed her in the side. "Oh," she said. "Yeah, they're really nice."

"We can also transfer images to mugs or refrigerator magnets or anything else you'd like," said the woman. "The process is very simple. Or you can paint all kinds of pottery items, if you prefer. Are you interested in making something today?"

George opened her mouth, about to answer the woman's question, but luckily, Bess cut her off. I was certain that George would have said no, that she wasn't interested, and I was glad Bess didn't give her that chance.

"Perhaps another time," said Bess quickly. Then she turned to me and George and said, "Mrs. Park has agreed to tell us where Beverly DeSantos lives, since we're such big fans of hers."

"Oh!" I said. "Yes, thank you."

Mrs. Park began walking back over to the front counter. I followed her while Bess and George hung back.

"Just as long as you promise to only walk past the

house," Mrs. Park said over her shoulder. "Please don't bother poor Beverly. She hates the attention. She's very private, you know."

"Of course," I said. I turned around, and Bess and I made eye contact for a moment, both clearly feeling guilty about this lie. Bothering Beverly was exactly what we planned to do. I just had to hope our meddling would eventually benefit Beverly DeSantos more than it would hurt her.

Mrs. Park pulled out a pen and a piece of paper from underneath the counter. She began writing down the address and a few quick directions with a shaky hand. "Beverly grew up here in Shady Oaks, you see. I've known her since she was a small girl," she said. "People here are so hard on her. Everyone always assumes the worst. She really doesn't deserve it."

"I'm sure she doesn't," I said. I was surprised that I actually meant this. I didn't think Beverly deserved all the hostility she got, though I wasn't completely sure why.

Mrs. Park finished writing and handed the slip of paper over to me. "Here you are," she said.

"Thank you," I told her. "You've really helped us."

Mrs. Park nodded at me and smiled. I turned away from the counter and headed back toward Bess and George.

"All right," I said. "Let's head over to Beverly's house and—"

Before I could say anything else, Bess called out, "Riley!" She said it loud enough to drown out what I was saying, and when I looked at her, I could see she was looking over my shoulder and waving.

I turned around and sure enough, Riley had just walked into the store. With the photographic warning, it was clear someone was watching the investigation. And I really wasn't sure who I could trust. I certainly couldn't tell anyone else that I was about to visit Beverly DeSantos, and for a moment I was worried about sneaking away from Riley long enough to go through with my plan.

"Hey, guys!" called Riley. "I saw you from outside."

She began walking toward us. "George," I whispered quickly. "Show Riley the dog plates."

"What?" said George, looking confused. "Why?"

Before I could answer, Riley was already standing next to us. For a moment, George didn't say anything. I nudged her shoulder.

"Um," said George. "Riley. Come look at these cool dog plates with me."

It wasn't the smoothest distraction ever. Bess and I both smiled as if nothing was wrong, and even though Riley looked a bit skeptical, she eventually said, "Okay. That sounds . . . interesting."

George and Riley headed in the direction of the wall of plates, and I pulled Bess farther away from them.

"I have to go visit Beverly," I whispered to her. "But I don't think we should tell anyone."

"Got it," Bess whispered back, and gave me a serious nod. "But please be careful. I'll make up something to tell Riley."

"Thanks, Bess," I said.

I stepped back outside. It was raining steadily now, and I pulled my hood up over my head. I looked over Mrs. Park's directions, which were fairly simple, and headed off to find Beverly DeSantos.

CHAPTER NINE

Some Better Lighting

THE WALK TO BEVERLY'S HOUSE WAS THE
farthest I'd had to travel since arriving in Shady Oaks.
It still wasn't too far, though, and it took me a little
over twenty minutes to get there. The rain was falling
heavily enough that it was pooling in the creases of my
raincoat and falling in thick droplets off the edge of
my hood.

At first I thought that I had somehow misread the
directions and ended up in a place where there wasn't
a house at all. Where Beverly DeSantos's house should
have been, all I could see were towering hedges. They

came all the way up to the edge of the sidewalk and were thick enough that I couldn't see through them. There was a small break in the middle of these bushes, though, and it was only when I peeked through this gap that I could see the house hiding behind them.

I walked past the hedges to the long driveway and up toward the front of the house. It was a large, modern-looking house that appeared nearly flat from this angle. The house was made almost entirely of windows. But heavy curtains covered them all so no one could see in—or out. I wondered why anyone would buy a house with that many windows if they only intended to cover them all up.

As I got closer to Beverly's front door, I began to feel more and more nervous. What if my hunch about her was actually wrong? Why hadn't I found a way to bring Bess and George along with me? Was it possible that I was walking up to the house of a kidnapper alone?

Standing in front of the large front door, I took a deep breath. I just had to trust my instincts. I raised my hand and knocked three times.

Almost immediately I heard someone shuffling around inside. I could hear whoever it was come up to the door and then stop without opening it. I had to assume it was Beverly, and I also had to assume she was looking out at me through some kind of peephole, or maybe with the help of a security camera.

After a moment, the door slowly opened. But it opened only a little. Beverly DeSantos probably didn't get many visitors, and it seemed like she didn't know how to react.

"Hello!" I said, trying my best to sound cheerful. "My name's Nancy and I'm a reporter. I was wondering if I could ask you a few questions?"

I was smiling wide, and I hoped it didn't look too fake. Beverly looked out at me from behind her door. Her expression implied that I had said something very strange, and I had the sudden feeling she did not believe anything I had just told her.

"Questions about what?" Beverly asked, still half-hidden in her doorway.

"Years ago, there was an article published about

you and your grandfather," I said, thinking quickly. "It made a lot of his fans upset. But I believe the article twisted your words, and now I want to write a new piece that clears your name."

There was a pause as Beverly seemed to be considering my words. Then she pulled away from me. "No," she said. "I don't answer questions about my grandfather anymore."

She leaned away from the doorframe, and I got a quick glimpse of the inside of her home. It was relatively simple, but the one thing I noticed was that the walls were covered in photographs. I didn't have enough time to get a good look at them, but they appeared to be family portraits. There was also one large photograph, hanging just behind Beverly's head and over the fireplace. It was of Christopher DeSantos and what appeared to be a young Beverly. They were both laughing.

Beverly began shutting the door and I cried, "Wait!"

Without thinking about it, I also stuck my foot in between the door and the doorframe. I knew this was a strange and rather rude thing to do, but I had to speak to Beverly for just a moment longer. I was now certain that the article I had read had been wrong about Beverly DeSantos. Who would keep a large portrait of someone they hated hanging in their home?

"Someone is sabotaging your grandfather's exhibit," I said quickly. I couldn't be sure how much time Beverly would give me to explain myself. "I'm not a reporter, I'm an amateur detective. I can figure out who is behind all this. But only if you help me."

My voice had lost all the fake cheeriness I had been using when I spoke earlier, and I knew this new approach was risky. But Beverly had seemed to see through all my attempts at covering up what I was really doing there, and telling her the truth seemed like the best option.

Beverly didn't say anything. Instead she just looked down at where my foot was blocking her door and then back up at my face. Her eyes were narrowed behind her thick curtain of bangs, and she looked as if she was deeply suspicious of me.

"You don't think I'm sabotaging the exhibit?" she asked me. She said it in a very neutral tone of voice, the way you might ask someone about the weather.

I shook my head. I was almost certain Beverly had nothing to do with what was going on. But I hoped she could help me find the real culprit.

Beverly leaned back from the doorway, and for a moment I thought she was going to try and shut the door again, whether my foot was in the way or not. But instead she swung the door wide open and gestured me inside.

"Thank you," I said, giving her a tentative smile as I stepped inside.

From the outside, Beverly's house had looked as though it would be a dark and cold space. I assumed that there would be curtains drawn over all the windows in the entire house, and that those tall hedges would block out most of the sunlight. But as I stepped inside, I could see that that wasn't actually the case. The curtains were much more sheer than I would have guessed, and they let in a soft, hazy kind of light. I guessed they both illuminated and protected the photographs on Beverly's walls. Everything was much more cozy and welcoming than I had anticipated.

I had also been right about the photographs on the walls. They all appeared to be of Beverly, and Christopher DeSantos, and other people who I assumed were their various family members. Above Beverly's fireplace was the largest photograph of them all, the image I had seen of Beverly and her grandfather laughing together.

Looking around, I felt silly for how nervous I had been walking up to this house. I no longer felt nervous at all. If anything, I just felt bad for Beverly and the way everyone in this town treated her.

Beverly led me over to the center of the room, where there was a long gray couch and a few chairs. All the furniture in her house was modern and a bit artistic, but arranged in a way that made everything feel comfortable and inviting.

She gestured toward the couch and I sat down on the edge of it, not wanting to look too relaxed. Beverly took the chair opposite me and laced her fingers in her lap. She looked at me expectantly.

I wasn't really sure where to start. "Someone is trying to ruin your grandfather's exhibit," I began. "And I don't think it's you."

"So you've said," said Beverly. She still seemed guarded, and she was looking at me like she was unsure of what to think. I thought that I could understand why. Everyone in Shady Oaks had assumed so many bad things about Beverly; why would she think that I was any different?

I decided to start from the beginning. I told Beverly about being sent the newspaper article, about deciding to come to Shady Oaks and trying to figure out what had happened to Grace Rogers. I told her about Jacob going missing and his girlfriend Emily's story about Terry Lawrence and his ability to curse people. I told her what I knew about Christopher DeSantos and Terry Lawrence, which admittedly wasn't much.

I decided to leave out the part about how many

Shady Oak locals thought Beverly might be behind these kidnappings, or how many of them believed she might harm them if they helped me. It didn't feel like information Beverly needed to know. Unfortunately, she seemed to figure this part out anyway.

"Let me guess," she said, when I had finished speaking. "Everyone thinks it's me?"

I nodded slowly. "Sorry," I said, though I wasn't sure what I was apologizing for.

Beverly shrugged like this was just something she was used to. "You must have thought it was me at one point," she said. "I overheard you and your friends discussing the case, at the diner. Your red-headed friend in particular seemed quite certain I had something to do with everything that's been happening."

"That was Riley," I said, cringing a bit. "I had to consider all the possibilities. I hope you understand. Though I no longer believe you had anything to do with the missing people."

Beverly looked down at her lap and sat in silence

for a minute, as though she was deciding whether or not to say something. "I have a confession as well," she said at last. I sat up a bit straighter. What could Beverly possibly have to confess? "I was the one who sent you that newspaper clipping."

"You were? Why?"

Beverly looked up at me and then said, "I knew someone was sabotaging the exhibit, and I needed a detective to figure out who. I didn't write you a letter or sign my name because I didn't want anyone to know you were working with me. If they did, no one would have trusted you. I considered contacting you once you got into town. . . ."

"But then you overheard my conversation at the diner," I finished for her. "And you thought you were my number one suspect."

"I was upset enough that I no longer wanted your help," admitted Beverly. "I went to Susan later that day and tried to convince her to shut down the exhibit instead. But she won't let me out of my contract. I signed on for at least ten weeks of this. We were arguing about it the day we ran into you in that back hallway."

I hunched my shoulders and did my best not to look too guilty. "Yeah," I said. "I heard some of what you said. It sounded like you were maybe threatening Susan."

It was Beverly's turn to look a little embarrassed. "I let my frustrations get the better of me," she said. "I was trying to save my grandfather's name and reputation. But instead, this exhibit was just making things worse. There isn't a curse on my grandfather's work. It's all ridiculous."

"Can I ask what did happen with your grandfather and Terry Lawrence?" I said. I couldn't help but feel that the relationship between the two former partners was still important in some way.

But Beverly only shrugged. "It's not such an interesting story," she said. "Terry was always jealous of my grandfather. He tried to steal credit for a photograph in order to boost his career. Their friendship never recovered. That was all."

"Do you have any proof that your grandfather took that photo?" I asked.

Beverly looked unhappy. "If I had any proof," she said, "I would have showed people a long time ago."

"Everyone in town seems so suspicious of you," I said. "Is there any reason besides the article that would make them think you're behind all this?"

Beverly shook her head. "Ever since that interview came out," she said, "everyone thinks I didn't love my family. People in this town were so proud that my grandfather lived here, so that was always difficult for them. But really, I just don't like the attention. I'm not always very good at making friends with people. The things I say often get taken the wrong way, and I think I frighten people sometimes."

I nodded sympathetically. It looked as though my hunch about Beverly was correct, but I couldn't feel very happy about that at the moment.

"I meant what I said in the article," said Beverly. "I do sometimes wish I was born into another family. But not because I didn't love my grandfather." She glanced up at the portrait of her and Christopher DeSantos as she said this. "I donated the new exhibit as a kind of peace offering to my grandfather's fans. I also thought it might help ease some of the controversy surrounding what happened with him and Terry Lawrence. I thought it would give people something new to talk about. But now there are people missing and everyone is saying that the photographs are cursed. I don't know what to do."

I sat quietly and thought about everything. Really, all I had to go on at this point was Beverly's word. But I felt as though her story made sense, and I was beginning to trust her more than I trusted anyone else I had met so far in Shady Oaks.

"So," said Beverly. "Why is it that you came here? Earlier, you said you needed my help."

"Right," I said. "There's a door hidden behind a bookcase in the museum's staff hallway. What if the culprit hid both Grace and Jacob behind there?"

Beverly nodded. "It's certainly possible," she said.

"I've tried to get past that door," I continued. "But

it's locked by the same combination that opens the museum's front door."

I paused here to see if Beverly could understand what I was asking. She knew almost immediately. "You want me to give you the combination," she said.

"I know of only three people who have it," I said. "Susan, Grace Rogers, and you. I already asked Susan and she said no. So it has to be you."

Beverly stared at me and it appeared as though her guarded nature had returned. I felt a little uncomfortable under her gaze but did my best to return it. Eventually she stood and walked into another room.

I sat up straighter on the couch and leaned forward, trying to see where she had gone. Had she decided she didn't trust me after all? If that was true, I had no idea what I was going to do next.

But then she returned with paper and a pen. She leaned forward over the coffee table in between us and scribbled down four numbers. *5796.*

"I chose the combination," she said, as she gave me the piece of paper. "Susan changes it for each new exhibit. It's the last four digits of my grandfather's old phone number."

I knew the numbers probably weren't random, but I had been assuming they would mean something to Susan, not Beverly.

"Thank you," I said to her, trying to sound as earnest as possible.

Beverly still looked as though she wasn't quite sure about trusting me. "I just hope you can find those missing people," she said. "And figure out who's behind all this."

"Me too." I stood up to leave and took one last look around Beverly's house. Just before I reached her front door, I turned back around and said, "You have a lot of lovely photographs in here."

Beverly had been walking behind me. She turned back as well and said, "I've kept everything. All his photographs and the souvenirs from his travels he gave me. It makes me feel closer to him."

I thought I understood what Beverly meant. I

smiled at her and thanked her once more before heading out. Beverly shut the door carefully behind me.

I hadn't realized how much time I had spent at Beverly DeSantos's house, but upon leaving I realized that I must have been in there for a while. The sun was setting as I walked back to the Elder Root Inn. Luckily, it wasn't raining anymore, and once I had been walking for a few minutes my blood was warm enough that I didn't feel too cold. There were hardly any clouds blocking the evening sky, and after the sun had fully set, I could look up and see countless stars.

By the time I reached the hotel, it was fully dark outside. Bess, George, and Riley were sitting in the hotel lobby on the comfortable couches near the front desk, and they appeared to be talking and laughing. Eventually Bess spotted me walking toward them.

"Nancy!" she called. "How was the visit with your aunt?"

I reached the couches and sat down, balancing on

one of the armrests. At first I had no idea what Bess was talking about. But then I remembered she had said she was going to think of a cover story for me, something to tell Riley. That must have been what she came up with.

"Oh," I said. "Yeah, she's great. It went really great."

Bess and George both grinned at me. They clearly understood that I meant my conversation with *Beverly* had gone well, even if we couldn't discuss it in front of Riley.

The four of us spent a few more minutes hanging out in the lobby. Eventually, though, Riley yawned loudly and said that she was going to head upstairs and go to bed. She was just about to leave when I asked her to wait a moment.

"I wanted to ask you a favor," I said.

"Sure, Nancy," she said. "What is it?"

"I need to borrow your camera."

Riley's hands flew up to the camera that was perpetually hanging around her neck. I knew this was a big ask; it was probably the most precious thing

Riley owned. But I also really needed to borrow a film camera.

"Why?" asked Riley.

"I think I can figure out what's going on at the DeSantos exhibit," I said. "I can find the missing people and stop these recent events from tarnishing DeSantos's name. But I need your camera to do that."

Riley still looked reluctant to hand the camera over. But finally she lifted the strap up over her head. "Just be really careful with it, all right?" she said.

"I promise," I said. "I can give it back to you tomorrow. Thank you, Riley. I really appreciate it."

She nodded and began heading to her room again. When she reached the stairs, she turned back for one last look at her camera before disappearing.

"Nancy," said George. "What was that about?"

"Yeah," said Bess. "Why do we need Riley's camera?"

"Because I got the combination from Beverly," I said. "And we're sneaking into the museum. Tonight."

CHAPTER TEN

~

Night at the Museum

THE THREE OF US WAITED UNTIL IT WAS nearly midnight to be certain no one would be at the museum. We spent the time hanging around our hotel room. Bess was reading and George was on her laptop, though I wasn't sure what she could be doing without an Internet connection. I was studying Riley's camera and making sure I knew how it worked.

Once it was late enough, we set out on foot toward the museum. I had Riley's camera hanging around my neck, and it was bumping up against me as I walked. I could feel a kind of nervous energy fluttering near my heart. There were so many things that could still go wrong, and I couldn't help but consider each one of them. Someone could be at the museum, for some reason. Beverly could have just given me a fake code, so I would get out of her house and leave her alone. And I could be totally wrong about Grace and Jacob being trapped in the museum at all.

At night the Carlisle Museum looked much darker and spookier than it had during the day. All the repairs the old building needed looked much more apparent in the moonlight. They made the Carlisle look somewhat haunted.

I walked up to the front door of the museum and took a deep breath. My fingers were hovering just above the keypad, which was silver and looked as though it was nearly glowing. This was the moment of truth, and I could only hope that Beverly DeSantos actually trusted me enough to tell me the right code.

"Nancy?" said George, from off to my right. "What are you waiting for?"

I shook my head. "Nothing," I said. Pressing each

button with my index finger, I typed in *5-7-9-6*.

Each of the four lights on the keypad flashed green, and I could hear the satisfying *click* of the door unlocking.

"It worked!" said Bess.

I glanced at her and smiled. I felt just as surprised as she looked.

"Come on," I said. "Let's get inside before somebody sees us." I pushed open the door and we all slipped inside the museum's dark entryway.

It took a minute for my eyes to adjust. The museum had so many windows that there was no way we would be able to turn on any lights. Someone outside might see and my entire plan would be ruined. Instead we all just walked forward slowly. The light streaming in from the lampposts outside was just enough to see by.

"So what do we do first?" asked George. She was whispering, even though I wasn't sure it was entirely necessary. There wasn't anyone here, and no one would be able to hear us talking from outside.

Even so, I couldn't help but whisper back. "I want

one more look at the images of Grace, Jacob, and me," I said, heading past the front desk in the direction of the exhibit room. "Beverly's house was filled with photographs. Some were old and taken with film. Some were much newer and, I think, taken with a digital camera. I have a feeling that the photos of Grace and Jacob, and the one of me, had to have been taken with an old film camera, to match the quality of the rest of the photo so well."

Bess and George nodded, and we entered the exhibit space. "The image with Jacob is that one," said George, pointing off to the left side of the room.

"Great," I said. I walked over to the photograph and turned my phone's flashlight on. I hoped we were far enough from the windows that no one would spot it. I spent a minute looking at the photograph closely, then walked over to the one with Grace's picture in it and studied that one too. Finally I looked at the photograph with me in the background. I still didn't know much about photography, but I felt confident that the original DeSantos photos and the pictures of Jacob, Grace, and me must have been taken by a similar type of camera. The tone and the quality of the inserted images matched the rest of the photo so closely. Whoever had taken the pictures of the three of us would have to own an old film camera from around the same time period.

When I was satisfied, I turned the flashlight off and looked over to see that Bess had wandered off and was standing in front of one of the photographs. I walked over to her.

"What are you looking at?" I said in a low voice.

I remembered the photograph from a previous visit. It was of an empty street somewhere near the edge of town, or at least where the edge of town had been. Perched on a thin and scraggly tree was a bird, just lifting its wings and about to take flight.

"When I first met Lucas, I was looking at this photo," Bess said. "He said that capturing this moment was just pure luck. The bird started to take off at exactly the right time. But when I asked how he knew that, he said he was just assuming and quickly changed the subject."

I thought about it for a moment. "Lucas does study art history," I said. "Maybe he read it somewhere."

"Yeah," said Bess. "Maybe."

"Hey!" called George, in a whisper-shout. "Aren't we going through here?" She was standing near the STAFF ONLY hallway and had her hand on the door handle.

"Actually," I said, "there's one more thing." I walked over to where one of the security cameras was hanging from the ceiling and pointed up at it. I had thought there was something off about these cameras, but now I had George here to test that theory. "What do you think of these cameras, George?" I asked.

She walked over to stand next to me, then looked directly up at the underside of the video camera with her face scrunched up.

"Hang on," she said. "I need a better look."

She walked out of the room and soon returned with a chair she said was from the front desk. After placing it underneath the camera, she stood up on the chair and was high enough to be nearly eye level with the camera's blinking red light. She used her own phone's flashlight function to get a better look.

Eventually she shook her head. "If this is their camera," said George, "then their security system is ancient. It shouldn't even still be working."

"Is there a way to tell if it is?" I asked her.

Instead of responding, George hooked her finger on one of the wires coming out of the camera. To our surprise, the wire popped right off from where it had appeared to be leading into the ceiling.

"George!" said Bess. "Did you break that?"

"No," said George with a grin. "It's fake! Look, the end of the wire just attaches right back onto the ceiling, like a sticker. But it doesn't actually lead anywhere."

"What about the flashing red light?" I asked.

"The light is probably battery powered," George said. Then she tapped the side of the camera's body. It sounded hollow. "But there's almost nothing in here. There's no way this camera is recording anything."

This meant that Susan had been lying about the

security footage. Which meant that she had also lied about the police watching that footage. Anyone could be sneaking around this museum at night, and there wasn't any way for her or the police to know.

"Great," I said. "Thanks, George."

She hopped down off the chair, and Bess carried it back to where George had found it. I made my way over to the STAFF ONLY door and placed my hand on the door handle.

"Ready?" I asked, glancing at Bess and George behind me. They both nodded.

The staff hallway looked even more crowded in the dark. I pulled my phone out again for the flashlight, but we still had to keep our eyes down and step carefully to avoid tripping over anything. I could feel all the dust back here tickling my nose again.

When we reached the bookcase, I turned to Bess and George. "We'll have to squeeze through one at a time," I said. "And we should try to be as quiet as possible. We don't know who might be back here."

My two friends stood silently as I went first, sliding

in between the bookcase and the wall. The keypad above the door handle looked identical to the one on the outside of the building. I typed in Beverly's combination. I held my breath, but I didn't actually need to be nervous. Once again, there were the flashes of green light and the sound of the door unlocking.

"We're in!" I whispered back to Bess and George. At the edge of the bookcase, I could just make out Bess giving me a thumbs-up.

The door opened to the closed-off wing of the museum. I wasn't worried that anyone would be able to see light back here, so we all pulled up our phones' flashlights. The room was filled with what must have been statues or sculptures, all covered by large white sheets. There were also a number of boxes and crates stacked against the walls. Two doorways led out of the room: one was directly across from me, and the other was to my left. As I waited for Bess and George to come through the door behind me, I looked around and couldn't help but find it all very spooky.

Bess, apparently, agreed with me. As soon as she

stepped through the door, she said, "This place is really creeping me out."

"Same," I said back, as George came through the door next. "But don't forget to whisper."

Bess nodded, and I watched as she pulled out her pepper spray and held it in front of her. She noticed me watching her, so she shrugged and said, "What? It's come in handy before."

I couldn't really argue with that. I started to walk forward, when George whispered my name from where she was hunched near the wall on our right side. "Look at this," she said.

I made my way over to her and crouched down next to her. It was a rectangular vent, and when I looked through it, I had a clear view of the DeSantos exhibit. I raised Riley's camera to my left eye and looked through the vent. I smiled.

"Nancy?" asked George. "Why are you smiling? This is so creepy."

"Because," I said. "Look through Riley's camera."

George did, squinting. She looked back at me

and shook her head. "I don't get it," she said.

"This is how whoever is behind all this was taking photographs of the people visiting the exhibit," I said. "They were taking them through here. Except whoever they are messed my photograph up. Do you remember that vertical line running down my torso in my picture? Whoever took the picture must have accidentally caught a piece of this vent in the shot."

Bess knelt down next to us. She asked to take a look as well, and I passed the camera over to her. "Yeah, that's exactly what this looks like!" she said, with the camera pressed to her face.

"That's partly why I needed to borrow Riley's camera tonight," I said. "To see if I could find anything that looked similar to that line."

I took the camera back from Bess and snapped a quick photograph through the vent. I made sure to catch one of the vent's vertical lines in the image, so I could compare it to the picture of myself later.

I walked over to each of the doorways and looked through them. The one that had been directly in front of us was just as messy as the room we were standing in, filled with more crates and statues and white sheets. The doorway off to the left, on the other hand, was nearly empty.

"Let's try this one first," I said, pointing at the more cluttered hallway. I knew it would be more difficult to walk quietly if we went this way, but if I wanted to keep something or someone hidden, I would put as many obstacles in the way as possible. Maybe the kidnapper was thinking along those same lines.

As we walked, I began taking photographs of anything that looked interesting, just in case I needed evidence of this place later on. I didn't want to miss a thing. It was nearly impossible for us to make no noise at all. Every once in a while, one of us bumped into a crate or statue, and once George tripped over one of the sheets.

After a while, the hallway turned off to the left. As we rounded the corner, I looked as far down as I could see in the low light. It looked as through the hallway would eventually turn again, and I wondered if it just ended or if it made one large circle, connecting back to the first room we'd seen.

Closer to us, and on the right side of the hallway, I could also see the outline of a doorway. There were noises and what looked like the lights of flashlights or lanterns coming from within it. I could hear something that sounded like hushed voices. I gestured for Bess and George to stay very quiet.

We started walking forward slowly. Anyone could be in that room. It could just be Grace and Jacob, talking to each other or trying to find a way to escape. Or it could be Grace, Jacob, and their kidnapper. Or it could be multiple kidnappers. I braced myself for any possibility. Bess held her pepper spray up higher.

The three of us were standing as close to the doorway as we dared. We leaned back flat against the wall. Carefully, I leaned over and peeked around the doorframe.

It was Grace and Jacob. But they were . . . laughing? They didn't seem to be trapped at all.

I glanced around the room, looking for more clues

about what was going on here. There were two sleeping bags, and enough food to last at least a few days. They seemed to be talking and joking with each other, leaning up against the back wall. There was nothing keeping them here that I could see. It looked more like they were here for an extended sleepover than because they had been kidnapped and trapped.

I leaned back around the doorframe and looked over at Bess and George. "They seem . . . fine," I whispered. "I don't think they've been kidnapped."

"So what do we do now?" George whispered back. "Call the police?"

Calling the police did seem to be the best idea. I nodded at George and gestured back toward the exit, thinking that we could use the phone at the front desk. The three of us began to turn around, and I watched as Bess's foot twisted itself in one of the sheets collecting on the ground. She only tripped a little, but it was enough to make her step down too hard and too loudly.

The three of us froze.

"Who's there?" called Jacob from inside their room.

Neither Bess nor George said anything. Instead they both looked at me as if I might tell them what to do next. I wasn't sure what the best move would be, but I knew we couldn't let Grace or Jacob get away.

Both of them stepped out of the doorway. They took one look at the three of us, standing in the hallway, and before we could say anything, they both pushed past us and took off running down the cluttered hallway, back the way we'd come.

"Go that way!" I called out to Bess and George, pointing after Grace and Jacob. They both began running, but instead of joining them, I turned and began heading the other way.

Grace and Jacob had been moving quickly, both probably heading for the door behind the bookshelf. I didn't think we would actually be able to catch them just by running after them. But if this hallway really was a circle, maybe I could run around the other way and head them both off.

I ran as quickly as I was able, the sound of my feet echoing around me. I turned the corner at the end of the hallway, and just like I had seen through the doorway of the left side, this hallway was nearly empty. Grace and Jacob would have to run around crates and statues and sheets, but I could run straight through.

I reached the room at the end of the hall and didn't stop until I was standing right in front of the doorway behind the bookcase. I turned around and covered the door with my arms, just in time to see Grace and Jacob in the room as well and running toward me. The two of them turned around, about to head back in the other direction, when George and Bess entered the room. Bess had her arm held up in front of her.

"Don't even think about it," she said, standing with her feet shoulder-width apart and pointing her pepper spray directly at Grace and Jacob.

CHAPTER ELEVEN

~

Missing the Picture

BESS MANAGED TO KEEP GRACE AND JACOB from running off while George found a phone and called the police. As we waited for the police to arrive, I tried asking Grace and Jacob what they were doing back here, and why they had pretended to disappear into the DeSantos photographs. I still couldn't figure out what their motives had been, and why they were willing to hide out in a museum for days just to ruin the exhibit.

I attempted to ask them about their supposed kidnapping, and it seemed as though Jacob might have wanted to explain what was happening. He opened his mouth and was about to say something when Grace elbowed him in the ribs and shook her head. Jacob stopped talking immediately and didn't look at me or try speaking again until the police arrived.

I recognized the police officer as the same one I had seen that first morning in Shady Oaks, the one who had taken Susan and Emily in for questioning. He and his partner entered the room behind the bookcase and pointed their flashlights in our direction.

The officers brought all five of us in for questioning. Even after we had explained to them everything we knew, Bess, George, and I stuck around the station. I wanted to hear what Grace and Jacob had to say, and what the police officers thought of their story. This mystery just didn't feel solved yet.

The three of us were sitting in the waiting room of the police station. George was leaning into her palm with her eyes shut and her mouth open. Every once in a while she would wake up with a jump and then slowly fall back into an uneasy sleep. Bess had so far been managing to stay awake, but I noticed her eyelids were fluttering and growing heavy.

Eventually the police officer I recognized walked past where we were sitting in the waiting room. His name was pinned to his uniform and it read OFFICER JAMES PATTY.

"Officer Patty!" I called out to him. My sudden shout startled both Bess and George. They jumped in their seats and stared blearily in Officer Patty's direction. "We were wondering what happened with Grace and Jacob."

Officer Patty looked a little annoyed that we had stuck around. He took a deep breath and reluctantly took a seat in front of us.

"If I tell you three, will you all go home?" he asked us.

I nodded quickly.

"Your friends keep changing their story," Office Patty began. "First they told me they were trying to destroy the DeSantos exhibit, and then they told me they were trying to *help* the exhibit and that they were pulling this stunt to get the museum more publicity. They said they were acting alone, and then they said they had an accomplice. They even tried to tell me they were actually kidnapped, but they took that one back pretty quickly."

"Grace and Jacob aren't our friends," I said. "And also, I don't think they were acting alone."

Officer Patty frowned at me. "Why would you say that?"

"There's a picture of me in one of the DeSantos photographs too," I said. "I'm sure it was put there as a warning because I was trying to solve this case. But Grace and Jacob have been hiding in the museum the entire time I've been in town. So how would they know I was investigating at all?"

Officer Patty shrugged. "They could've figured it out," he said. "They could have . . . overheard something at the museum."

"True," I said, even though I didn't think that sounded very likely. "But you also said that they keep changing their story. I bet it's because someone else has been telling them what to do up until this point. Now that that person isn't around, they aren't sure how to act."

"Or they're just trying to figure out the best thing to say in order to get in the least amount of trouble," said Officer Patty. He leaned forward and placed his hands on his knees as he stood up.

"But—" I began. Officer Patty didn't give me the chance to say anything else, though.

"I don't know why you girls thought it was okay to try and solve this case yourselves," he said. "But the real detectives are taking over now, and we've already caught the people behind it. So I'm going to ask you three to go home and not interfere again."

Officer Patty gave us a stern look before walking away, farther into the police station. I looked toward Bess and George, and they seemed just as bothered by this interaction as I was. Hadn't we been the ones to catch Grace and Jacob? Really, though, there was nothing else for us to do. We eventually gathered up our things and headed outside.

I hadn't been paying attention to the time. So when we walked outside and saw that the sun was rising, I was caught by surprise.

"It's morning?" I said to Bess and George. "We stayed up all night?"

My two friends, it seemed, were very aware of how long we had been awake. Bess tried to give me a disbelieving look, but it was interrupted when she let out a large yawn. George rolled her eyes at me and said, "Yeah, Nancy. Aren't you tired?"

I was a little tired, but I also felt right on the verge of solving this mystery. I supposed the adrenaline was keeping me awake.

"So," said George. "We solved it, right? It was Grace and Jacob?"

I shook my head. "We have to be missing something," I said. "What was their motive? How did they get their own pictures into the photographs in the exhibit? And how did they know I was investigating them? I meant what I said to Officer Patty. I think there's someone else working with them, someone who was telling Grace and Jacob what to do. We just have to figure out who they are."

"How do we do that?" asked Bess. She was rubbing one of her eyes, and I could see how tired she was. I couldn't help but feel a rush of gratitude that both of my friends were still trying to solve this mystery with me, even as they were half-asleep.

I shook my head. "I don't know," I admitted.

"Maybe if you slept on it," said Bess.

"Yeah," said George. "Let's go back to the hotel. We'll get some sleep and pick this back up again in a few hours."

I looked at George quickly. "Wait!" I said. The mention of the Elder Root Inn had given me an idea, had reminded me of someone else who must have been involved in all this. "We should go back to the hotel. But not to sleep."

I took off down the sidewalk, and after a moment I could hear Bess and George behind me, jogging to catch up. George let out a groan.

"Nancy?" asked Bess. She didn't sound any happier

about suddenly having to run. "What are you talking about?"

"We have one more person to question," I said. "Jacob's girlfriend, Emily."

Bess, George, and I made it back to the hotel as quickly as we could, considering it was a fairly long walk and we were all running on such small amounts of sleep. Eventually we made it up to the second floor, and I remembered which room had been Emily's: room 212.

The three of us stood outside Emily's door and I knocked on it. Emily had said I could stop by if I ever had any more questions for her. But I was fairly certain she hadn't meant I could stop by this early in the morning. It wasn't even eight o'clock yet, and I wasn't sure if she would be awake.

To my surprise, the door opened and revealed that Emily was fully dressed. She looked nervous as she peeked out the door. But when she saw us, she breathed what appeared to be a sigh of relief.

"Nancy!" she said, her shoulders slumping. "Sorry,

I was expecting . . . Never mind." She shook her head. "Come in, come in. Quickly."

Emily gestured us all inside. In a direct contrast to how sleepy Bess and George were, Emily seemed to be full of energy. As soon as we were all in the room, she began rushing around the small space. It took me a moment to realize that the room wasn't just messy like it had been last time. This time, Emily was quickly packing.

"Are you leaving?" I asked her.

I stood in the middle of the room as Emily bustled around me. Bess and George found the only chair not covered in clothing, a cushioned one just underneath the window, and they both slumped down into it. They were practically sitting on top of each other, and they appeared to be half-asleep within seconds.

"Well," said Emily. "Yes. I'm leaving. Honestly, Nancy, I thought you were the police a few seconds ago, and I really can't talk to them."

"Emily, wait," I said. "Why can't you talk to the police?"

For a moment I wondered if Emily could be the one behind everything, the one telling Grace and Jacob what to do. But really, it just didn't seem likely. Emily had already offered me so much information about the case and had said she'd be happy to talk to me whenever. She seemed as though she had enjoyed all the attention she'd been receiving this week, but she just didn't seem malicious enough to stage a kidnapping and frame an innocent person.

"There's someone else involved in all this," she said. Her eyes widened, as if she was surprised by her own admission. "They'd be so mad at me if I said anything. They're already mad about Grace and Jacob getting caught by the police."

I felt a jolt of adrenaline running through me. I had been right about another person being involved, and Emily knew just who that other person was.

"Emily," I said, trying to keep my voice as steady as possible. "Who would be mad at you if you said anything to the police?"

Emily hadn't stopped moving since Bess, George,

and I had entered the room. Now she was nearly finished packing. She looked at me as she was zipping up her suitcase and said, "No way. Sorry, Nancy, but I can't tell you that."

I wasn't sure what to do. Emily was the only lead I had, and I had no idea how to convince her to tell me anything. Perhaps Emily was actually a fairly decent person who'd gotten wrapped up in something not very decent at all.

"Emily, please," I said. "This is really important." Then I remembered why she was even part of the recent events. "Jacob's your boyfriend," I said. "He and Grace are going to be blamed for all this unless I can figure out who else is behind those photographs."

Emily rolled her eyes. "Jacob is not my boyfriend," she said. "We just go to school together. I guess the original plan was only to have Grace go missing. They thought the police would shut down the exhibit immediately. But the police just thought it was a hoax, and no one in town really cared because Grace hadn't been here for that long and no one knew anything about her. It was easy for everyone to believe that she had just gone back to where she came from. So Jacob was going to pretend to go missing too. He hoped it would scare more people in town if they thought the curse could apply to anyone who even went near the photographs, not just the people involved in displaying them. And this time they also wanted someone to hype everyone up about it."

"And that's where you came in," I supplied.

Emily nodded. "I'm a theater major. They needed someone who could act scared and hopefully frighten everyone in town enough that the police would be forced to act as soon as possible."

"Emily, why would you go along with this?" I asked. "It seems like a huge risk for you."

"Jacob said he could pay me," said Emily, shrugging. "He said something about a will, and that he would have plenty of money once this was all done. I have student loans to think about, and this is sort of an acting gig, so I said yes."

"A will? Whose will?"

Emily pulled her suitcase down from where it had

been resting on her bed. Her hand was wrapped around the handle, and she was just about ready to leave the room and end our conversation.

"I really can't say anything," she said, shaking her head. She actually did look sorry about it. "But I can give you a hint."

At this point, I was willing to take anything I could get. "Of course," I said. "Anything."

Emily looked around, as if there was someone who could possibly overhear us. I wasn't even sure if Bess and George were listening to us at this point, they were both so out of it.

"The person who set all this up, they wrote their name down somewhere," said Emily. "It's the only trail that they've left, that I know of anyway."

"They wrote their name down?" I clarified. "Where?"

"Have you been to the local arts and crafts store here in town?" Emily asked. "It's run by a woman named Mrs. Park."

"Actually, yes," I said, surprised at the coincidence.

"Well, the person behind all this did a project at

that store," said Emily. "And you have to sign your name in order to make anything there. So they did."

At first I didn't say anything. If Emily didn't sound so serious while she was telling me all this, I would have thought she was joking. What did Mrs. Park and the local arts and crafts store have to do with a fake kidnapping? It just didn't seem possible.

Emily must have sensed my hesitation, because she began repeating herself. "Seriously, Nancy," she said. "The arts and crafts store. Go talk to Mrs. Park. It's really important."

I nodded once, to let Emily know that I believed her. I was still confused by the whole thing, but she seemed so earnest, and I wanted to convey that I did, in fact, trust her.

"Thank you, Emily," I said. "Really, you've been a big help."

She gave me a brief smile before pulling up the handle on her rolling suitcase. "Bye, Nancy," she said as she walked out the door and into the hallway. "Good luck."

CHAPTER TWELVE

Hiding in Plain Sight

AFTER EMILY HAD HURRIED AWAY DOWN the stairs, I gently shook Bess and George awake. I told them what Emily had said, and that we had to go visit Mrs. Park and her store immediately.

George yawned loudly and Bess shook her head.

"Nancy, nothing in this town opens until at least nine o'clock," said Bess. "There's no way the arts and crafts store is open yet."

"Yeah," said George. "And anyway, we all need to *sleep*."

As much as I wanted to figure out what Emily

had been trying to tell me, it was pretty difficult to argue with either of them. The store probably wasn't open yet, and I had already made Bess and George stay awake for far too long.

"Okay, you're both right," I said. I held out my hands and helped them to their feet. "Let's go back to our room. You've both earned a long nap."

Bess smiled at me gratefully. George had already trudged past me, well on her way toward her bed.

Back in our room on the third floor, Bess and George fell into their beds without even changing their clothes. They were both asleep almost immediately, and the sound of George softly snoring filled the room.

I lay down on my bed and tried to sleep as well, but I just couldn't manage it. I couldn't talk to Mrs. Park yet, or ask to see her records, but I could go through every other piece of information I had.

I also still had Riley's camera. I had taken it off when we entered our hotel room, and now it was resting on my stomach. I kept turning it over and over in my hands, wishing that the camera were digital. If it were, then I would already be able to see all the photographs I had taken at the museum. I wanted to scan them for any potential clues I had missed in the moment.

I set Riley's camera on the nightstand next to me. There really wasn't any use in just holding it and wishing I could see the images inside.

Instead I pulled out my cell phone. I still didn't have any service, so I couldn't do any research on the Internet. I flipped through some of my old messages. I had forgotten about everything George had sent to me yesterday morning, when we were in the local coffee shop. I opened up the files one by one, until I came to the photograph of a young Christopher DeSantos and a young Terry Lawrence, posing with their arms around each other's shoulders.

Now that the image was on my phone, I could zoom in and peer at all the details I hadn't been able to see before. I remembered what Beverly had told me, that she had kept some of her grandfather's trinkets and souvenirs from his travels. She had said that it helped her feel closer to him. Both he and Terry

Lawrence were covered in pieces of jewelry and other objects that could be considered trinkets. As I focused in on Christopher DeSantos, I couldn't help but wonder which of these items Beverly still owned.

I swiped over to look more closely at Terry Lawrence. He had on a beaded necklace and that triangle-shaped earring I had noticed the first time I glanced at this photograph. I zoomed in as far as I could on his earring. . . .

I sat up and gasped. Quickly I began shaking Bess and George awake. They had only been asleep for a couple of hours, and I did feel bad about waking them up so soon. But this was just too important to wait.

The more I shook George's shoulder, the more she buried her face into her pillow and pretended to ignore me.

Bess, on the other hand, managed to sit up slowly. She stretched and said, "What's going on, Nancy?"

"We have to go see Mrs. Park at the arts and crafts store," I said. "Now."

"But why?" mumbled George, her voice muffled by the pillow.

"I think I've just figured this whole thing out," I said. "But we have to talk to Mrs. Park to be absolutely sure."

After a little more coaxing, I managed to get both Bess and George awake and out the door. By the time we reached Mrs. Park's store, she was only just opening up for the day. I watched as she bent down to prop her front door open.

"Mrs. Park!" I called from a little ways down the street. I jogged in her direction. Bess and George, who were now much more awake and starting to grow more and more curious about what exactly I had figured out, followed closely behind.

"Oh, hello, girls," said Mrs. Park from behind her large glasses. "Are you here to do a project today?"

"Not exactly," I said. "Actually, I was wondering if we could speak a bit more privately. Inside, maybe?"

Mrs. Park seemed a little confused by this request. "Well, sure, dear," she said anyway, turning around and walking toward her front counter. Once she reached it, she turned back around to face us and said, "What can I do for you three?"

I wasn't really sure what to ask. Emily had said that Mrs. Park kept records of anyone who had made a project at her store. But I was also sure that those records wouldn't be available for just anyone to look through.

In the end, I decided the best thing to do was just to dive in. After all, Mrs. Park had told us where Beverly DeSantos lived. It was possible she would be willing to share this information with us as well.

"Mrs. Park," I said, "I was wondering if we could take a look at your records. We need to find the name of someone who once made a project here. It's very important." At the last minute, I also decided to add, "It's to help Beverly DeSantos."

Mrs. Park scrunched up her face and shook her head. "Of course I'd want to help Beverly," she said. "But I think I'd feel strange just handing over the names of my customers like that. You understand."

"Please, Mrs. Park," I tried again. "You're the only one who can help us."

Mrs. Park was firm in her answer. "I just don't think it would be right," she said. "Sorry, dear." She patted my shoulder kindly, sat down, and began shuffling through some of the papers lying around her work space.

I let out a deep breath and turned back to Bess and George, feeling defeated.

"All right, Nancy," said Bess. "Now you have to tell us. What's going on?"

"Yeah," said George. "And why couldn't we have kept sleeping for a few more hours?"

I nodded. My friends were right: they deserved to know what was going on.

First I walked over to the dog plates hanging on Mrs. Park's wall. "Emily said this store was important, right?" I began. "And that whoever was behind this did a project here. Well, I actually think they did three projects here."

Bess and George stepped closer and looked at the plates. For a moment, they didn't seem to understand what I was trying to tell them. But eventually Bess's eyes lit up.

"Oh!" said Bess. "You think that whoever is behind this imprinted the modern-day images onto the DeSantos photographs in the same way Mrs. Park makes her plates."

"Exactly," I said. George stepped forward and ran her fingers over the images on the plates as I explained a bit more. "I looked it up, and it's an easy enough process. You just cover the photograph with a certain type of glue, and the image transfers to the glue. When it dries, you carefully remove any paper on the back of the photo, and you have what's essentially a decal, which you can stick on any surface."

"But Nancy," said George, "how would anyone manage to sneak one of the DeSantos photographs out of the museum? Wouldn't Susan notice that a piece of her exhibit was missing? Or wouldn't Mrs. Park realize there was a priceless piece of art in her store?"

The three of us looked in Mrs. Park's direction. She had lifted up her glasses and was squinting at a piece of paper in her hands. She was clearly having trouble seeing it well enough to actually read it.

"Okay, maybe she wouldn't have noticed," conceded George. "But still, getting one of those photographs out of the museum would be really difficult."

I shook my head. "I don't think the photographs ever left the museum," I said. "Whoever did all this could have just stuck the picture of me or Grace or Jacob on any piece of glass. As long as it was the same size as the photograph's picture frame, they could just sneak into the museum at night and switch out the pieces of glass."

"Isn't there a lock on each of the picture frames, though?" asked Bess. "How would whoever was doing this know those combinations?"

"My guess is the combination on the picture frames is the same one Susan uses for the museum's doors," I said. "Whoever knew that combination could mess with any of the photographs they wanted."

"So it has to be someone with that combination," said George. "It has to be Susan, Beverly DeSantos, or Grace. But how do we know which one?"

"Actually," I said, "I don't think it was any of them.

Grace knew the combination, so she could have just told whoever she was working with."

"So it could still be anyone," said George, looking frustrated.

"I don't think so," I said. "I think I know who it is. And it was something Bess said that first made me suspicious of this person."

"Me?" said Bess. "What did I say?"

"Remember last night, when we were in the museum and you and I were looking at that photograph of a bird about to take flight?"

Bess nodded.

"You told me that Lucas said that photograph was a moment of pure luck," I continued. "I suppose he could have just read that somewhere, but I couldn't help but wonder if he had learned it somewhere else. And then, while you were both sleeping, I looked at that old photograph of Terry Lawrence and Christopher DeSantos. The one you found, George, before their big falling-out. And look . . ."

I pulled out my phone and quickly found the image

I was talking about. I once again zoomed in as much as possible on Terry Lawrence and his triangle-shaped earring.

"Look familiar?" I asked them.

At first Bess just shook her head. George looked similarly stumped by my question. But then Bess's jaw dropped open and she said, "His earring is a shark tooth!"

I smiled at her. "Exactly," I said.

"A shark tooth?" asked George, grabbing my phone and bringing it as close to her face as she could manage. "What does that mean? What am I missing here?"

"Not just any shark tooth," I said. "It's one we've all seen before. Because now, Lucas wears it as a necklace."

George looked up, eyes wide, from where she was staring at my phone.

"When I visited Beverly DeSantos," I continued, "she told me that she keeps trinkets from her grandfather in order to feel closer to him. What if Lucas does the same thing?"

"Because Lucas is Terry Lawrence's grandson?" asked Bess tentatively.

I nodded, glad that my friends were thinking along the same lines that I was. "Remember that obituary we read for Terry Lawrence?" I said. "It said he had three grandchildren."

"Lucas, Grace, and Jacob," said George slowly. "You're saying that they planned this whole thing together because they're Terry Lawrence's grandchildren?"

"I think so," I said. "Emily told us that Jacob said he could pay her once this was all over, with the money he would get from someone's will. Maybe there was something in Terry Lawrence's will about keeping the idea of the curse alive."

"Plus," said Bess, "Lucas was the only one here in town who immediately knew who you were, Nancy. He said that he'd read about you solving cases before. So he probably knew that you were here to solve this case from the moment he saw you. It could explain why he was so eager to be friends with us."

I hadn't thought about that. I looked at Bess and hoped this information didn't hurt her feelings, since she was closer to Lucas than either me or George. She didn't look upset, though. She looked a little surprised by all this new information, but more than anything she looked pleased to have some answers and to have helped solve a piece of this mystery.

"So what now?" asked George. "What evidence do we have?"

I looked back over to where Mrs. Park was still sitting at the front counter. "I was really hoping to see Mrs. Park's records," I said. "Emily said that Lucas had written his name down here. It would be the most concrete piece of evidence we have. Especially if he wrote down what kind of project he was working on."

The three of us thought about this for a moment, before Bess got a determined look in her eye and began walking back in Mrs. Park's direction.

"What is she doing?" George whispered to me, but I could only shrug in response. Mrs. Park had already told us that she couldn't help us.

When Bess reached the front desk, she said, "Hi, Mrs. Park," in a sweet tone of voice.

George and I looked at each other and then hurried after her. We stood on either side of Bess and leaned up against the counter.

"Hi, dear," said Mrs. Park. "But like I told your friend, I just can't let you see my records."

"No, I know," said Bess. "That's okay. But maybe you could just tell us, did a boy named Lucas ever come in here? Maybe he did a photography project, something like the nice plates you have on your wall?"

Mrs. Park was fidgeting and looking a little uncomfortable about answering the question. But eventually she seemed to give in. "I suppose there's no harm in answering that question," she said. "Yes, he did. He came in a few different times, as a matter of fact. Three times, I believe."

CHAPTER THIRTEEN

~

A New Exhibit

AFTER PUTTING TOGETHER ALL THE CLUES we'd gotten in Mrs. Park's arts and crafts store and finally figuring out who was behind the mysterious photographs, the three of us rushed over to the police station to find Officer Patty. It took a little convincing to get him to listen to us, but once he heard everything we had to say, he had no choice but to bring Lucas in for questioning.

As soon as they saw Lucas entering the police station, Grace and Jacob immediately caved and told the police officers everything. They must have known there was no way out for them, now that Lucas had been caught. The two of them told Officer Patty that they were all cousins, the last living descendants of Terry Lawrence. They told him how it had all been Lucas's idea. There *had* once been a fire in a museum that had housed some of DeSantos's photographs, but all of the incidents after that, the missing people and the museums shutting down, had just been rumors started by Terry Lawrence. In his will, Lawrence even set aside a sum of money for any of his family members willing to keep the idea of the curse alive.

The police held Lucas, Grace, and Jacob overnight. Bess, George, and I went back to the hotel for some well-deserved rest. Almost as soon as we made it back to the Elder Root Inn, Bess and George were in their beds and fast asleep. The lack of sleep had finally caught up with me as well, and I couldn't help but follow soon after them.

The next morning I told Bess and George that I wanted to stop by the police station one last time. I was eager to know what would happen to Lucas, Grace, and Jacob now that they had confessed. My two friends said they would meet me at the museum whenever I had finished speaking to Officer Patty.

By the time I left the police station, the sun was peeking through the heavy clouds that had been hanging over Shady Oaks for most of the morning. I took my time walking in the direction of the museum. It was one of the first strolls through Shady Oaks where I could really enjoy the town and all its fall foliage. I had my red raincoat on once more, though I really didn't feel as though I needed it, and Riley's camera was still hanging around my neck. I hadn't yet had a moment to find her and give it back to her.

I reached the Carlisle Museum and noticed that Susan and Beverly were standing outside and pointing toward some of the more run-down sections of the building. Even from a distance, I could tell that their relationship was looking much less strained than it had been in the past. Susan seemed much happier to be speaking to Beverly, and Beverly was even smiling. Well, as much as I imagined Beverly DeSantos ever smiled.

I waved at them both as I approached the museum.

"Nancy!" said Susan. "Come to take one last look at the DeSantos photographs?"

"Sort of," I said. Really, I was there to meet Bess and George, but I supposed I could take a final look around.

"Well, get your fill of these photographs, and then make sure to come back in the spring," said Susan. "Beverly here has just agreed to donate an entirely new exhibit, as a permanent installment."

"Wow," I said. "Really?" I looked toward Beverly as I said this. After her experience with this first exhibit, and with the way I knew she felt about being in the public eye, I was surprised she was willing to donate more of her personal photographs.

Beverly shrugged. "I think it's what my grandfather would have wanted," she said. "And if someone tries to sabotage the exhibit again, we can just call you." She said this lightheartedly, and I couldn't help but smile back at her.

Before I could really respond, however, Susan

began speaking again. "That's not all," she said. "With the publicity the museum's received from this whole debacle, we've made enough money to reopen the closed sections of the museum! I'm going to make the DeSantos photographs that were tampered with a permanent exhibit. People love looking at them!"

"Oh," I said. "Great." Memorializing a faked curse didn't seem like a very good idea to me, but it didn't feel like my place to say anything.

It appeared that Beverly felt the same way I did. I watched as she rolled her eyes behind Susan's back. So maybe their working relationship wasn't entirely fixed.

"Hey," I said. "Have you seen my friends Bess and George anywhere? I was supposed to be meeting them."

Both Susan and Beverly shook their heads. I thanked them anyway and then peeked inside the museum. They weren't there. Then I looked around the front entryway before heading back outside. They were nowhere to be found. For a moment I became worried that perhaps this whole case wasn't really over, that now my friends were missing. But then I spotted them just around the corner from the museum, sitting at the park picnic bench where George and I had once spent some time talking.

I began heading in their direction, and Bess waved to me over George's shoulder. George turned around and waved at me as well.

"Were you just talking to Susan and Beverly?" Bess asked once I was in earshot.

I nodded. I told them what Susan had said, about making the installations permanent. Both Bess and George looked conflicted over the idea that the images of fake missing people—including one of me—would now be hanging in a museum long term.

"That's . . . interesting," said Bess.

"And what about the police station?" asked George. "What did Officer Patty say?"

"Not much," I admitted. "He still didn't want to share too much information with me about what would happen to Lucas, Grace, and Jacob. But they have all confessed to faking the curse."

"What about the defacement of art?" said George. "Isn't that against the law?"

"Actually," I said, "Officer Patty did tell me that the photographs are fine. It was like I had guessed: Lucas transferred the images of me, Grace, and Jacob to three pieces of glass, which he then switched with the glass in each of the picture frames. The photographs were never touched."

Bess looked thoughtful, and then said, "Lucas did love photography. He didn't lie about studying historical photographs in school. Maybe he couldn't bring himself to ruin a photograph, in the end. Even if it was one taken by his grandfather's rival."

I couldn't help but wonder if this was another case of Bess attempting to find the best in someone, even when they didn't deserve it. I decided that perhaps this time I'd try to believe that she was right. "Yeah," I told her. "Maybe that's true."

Eventually the three of us stood and headed back in the direction of the Carlisle Museum. I did want to take one last look at the photographs before we left town.

As we were walking over, I spotted Riley and her red hair glowing in the sunlight. I called out to her and held up her camera so she could see it.

When we were close enough to each other, I handed the camera back over to her. "Thanks for letting me borrow this," I told her. "It was a huge help. Sorry I'm getting it back to you so late."

"That's all right!" said Riley. But I noticed she was holding on to her camera very tightly. She slipped it back over her neck and seemed instantly more comfortable, like it had perhaps been a part of her that was missing.

"Hey," I said. "Could I ask you for one more favor?"

Riley gripped her camera like I might try and take it from her again, but she still said, "Sure. What is it?"

"Would you mind taking a picture of me, Bess, and George? Just here, in front of the museum."

"Oh!" said Riley. "Of course." She looked relieved that I hadn't tried to separate her from her camera again. "How about over there?"

The three of us headed in the direction that Riley

had been pointing and posed with our arms around each other. Riley took a few photographs before I had another idea.

Susan had disappeared inside, but Beverly was still standing off to the side of the museum, looking up at the potential work to be done.

"Hey, Beverly," I said, jogging over to her. "Would you take a picture with us? Only if you want to." Beverly had so many happy photographs of herself and her family. I wondered how long it had been since she'd last taken a photograph like that, and if she would want to take one with us now.

Beverly thought about my question for a moment, before smiling brightly and walking over to join us.

I MEANT WHAT I SAID TO SUSAN AND
Beverly. When they opened their new Christopher
DeSantos exhibit in the spring, I was eager to drive
back to Shady Oaks and see it for myself!

Ned and I made a fun day trip of it, staying long
enough to take a good look at all the new photographs. I even showed Ned the image of me trapped
in a DeSantos photograph, which was still hanging up at the Carlisle. Now that the mystery behind
the photograph was solved, it was pretty cool to see
it again. But I think I've had my fill of mysterious
photographs for a while!

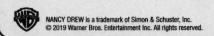